CHILDREN'S THRIFT CLASSICS

The Hunchback of Notre Dame

VICTOR HUGO

Abridged by Bob Blaisdell
Illustrated by Thea Kliros

DOVER PUBLICATIONS, INC.
New York

DOVER CHILDREN'S THRIFT CLASSICS
EDITOR OF THIS VOLUME: CANDACE WARD

Published in Canada by General Publishing Company, Ltd., 30 Lesmill Road, Don Mills, Toronto, Ontario.
Published in the United Kingdom by Constable and Company, Ltd., 3 The Lanchesters, 162–164 Fulham Palace Road, London W6 9ER.

Bibliographical Note

This Dover edition, first published in 1995, is a new abridgment of a standard text of an English translation of *Notre-Dame de Paris*. The illustrations and the introductory Note have been specially prepared for this edition.

Library of Congress Cataloging-in-Publication Data

Hugo, Victor, 1802–1885.
  The hunchback of Notre Dame / Victor Hugo ; abridged by Bob Blaisdell ; illustrated by Thea Kliros.
    p.   cm. — (Dover children's thrift classics)
  Summary: A retelling of the tale, set in medieval Paris, of Quasimodo, the hunchbacked bellringer of Notre Dame Cathedral, and his struggles to save the beautiful gypsy dancer Esmeralda from being unjustly executed.
  ISBN 0-486-28564-2 (pbk.)
  1. France—History—Medieval period, 987–1515—Juvenile fiction.
[1. France—History—Medieval period, 987–1515—Fiction. 2. Notre-Dame de Paris (Cathedral)—Fiction. 3. Physically handicapped—Fiction. 4. Paris (France)—Fiction.] I. Blaisdell, Robert. II. Kliros, Thea, ill. III. Hugo, Victor, 1802–1885. Notre-Dame de Paris. English. IV. Title. V. Series.
PZ7.H8745Hu   1995
[Fic]—dc20   95-17673
                                                                                  CIP
                                                                                  AC

Manufactured in the United States of America
Dover Publications, Inc., 31 East 2nd Street, Mineola, N.Y. 11501

Note

VICTOR HUGO (1802–1885), son of an army officer, spent much of his childhood traveling throughout Napoleon's empire. He considered Paris his true home, however, and the years from 1815 to 1818 were spent in study there. Though Hugo later spent time studying law, his literary ambitions prevailed. His first book of poetry, *Odes et poésies diverses* (1822), earned him a pension from King Louis XVIII.

In 1831 one of Hugo's greatest literary works was published. *The Hunchback of Notre Dame,* though an intricately detailed historical novel, has endured because the stories of Quasimodo, Claude Frollo and Esmeralda are so compelling. The present volume retells the basic story of Hugo's classic, highlighting the adventure, suspense and romance of the original in a way that is sure to enthrall young readers.

Contents

List of Illustrations

I

The Feast of Fools

ON JANUARY 6, 1482, the people of Paris were waked by the sound of loud peals from all the bells within the city. The day was a double festival, of Epiphany (the last of the twelve days of Christmas) and the Feast of Fools, to be celebrated with fireworks, a play and other festivities.

Crowds of Parisians were making their way from every quarter toward the Palace of Justice, where the play was to be performed. Shouts, laughter and the tramp of countless feet made a great noise and hubbub.

The play was written by a poor young poet, a tall, thin man with bright eyes and a smiling mouth—Pierre Gringoire. As happens even nowadays, the audience was far more interested in the costumes of the actors than in the speeches they recited; and, to tell the truth, they were quite right, as the play was quite bad.

Halfway through, a noisy guest from Flanders interrupted the play, saying, "This is not what I was told I should see; I was promised a Feast of Fools and the election of the Fools' Pope. This is how we do it in Ghent. We collect a crowd, as you do here; then every man in his turn puts his head through a window and makes a face at the rest; he who makes the ugliest face is chosen pope by

1

popular acclaim. It's very amusing. Would you like to choose your pope after the fashion of my country? At least it would be better than listening to those chatterboxes on stage. If they will come and make their faces through the window, they can join the game. What say you, Sir Citizens?"

This proposal was greeted with enthusiasm. Indeed, each year on the day of the Feast of Fools, the people were allowed to mock Church politics. They could elect a pope of their own of whom they could make fun, without fear of punishment.

In the twinkling of an eye, all was ready for carrying out the guest's idea. The little chapel in the hall opposite the stage was chosen as the site. A broken window pane above a door served as the setting through which the contestants should thrust their heads. To reach the window, they had to climb upon a couple of barrels. All candidates, men or women, so that the effect of their funny faces should not be weakened, covered their faces and remained hidden in the chapel until the proper moment to appear. In less than an instant the chapel was filled with contestants.

The contest began. The first to appear at the window, with eyelids inside out so they showed the red, a gaping mouth and a wrinkled forehead, produced great laughter. A second, a third comical face followed, then another, and another; and still the shouts of laughter and stampings of delight increased.

"Oh, my goodness!"

"Just look at that face!"

"That's nothing!"

"Let's have another!"

"Hurrah! Hurrah!" shouted the people on all sides.

And then the most miraculously ugly face of all

appeared at the hole in the window. We will not try to give the reader any idea of that four-sided nose, of that horseshoe-shaped mouth; of that small left eye overhung by a bushy red eyebrow, while the right eye was completely hidden by a monstrous wart; of those uneven, broken teeth, with sad gaps here and there; of that thick lip, over which one of these teeth projected like an elephant's tusk; of that forked chin; and especially of the expression on this face—a mixture of spite, amazement and sadness.

Everyone voted for this contestant; the crowd rushed into the chapel. They returned leading the lucky Fools' Pope in triumph. But it was then only that surprise and admiration reached its highest; the expression which had so amused them was his real face.

He had a large head bristling with red hair; between his shoulders an enormous hump, with a corresponding bulge in front; legs and thighs so crooked that they touched only at the knees; broad feet, huge hands; and, in spite of all this deformity, an awe-inspiring look of strength, agility and courage. He looked like a giant who had been broken to pieces and badly cemented together. This was the pope whom the fools had chosen to reign over them.

Now that he appeared upon the threshold of the chapel, the people recognized him instantly, by his red and purple coat and particularly by his ugliness, and cried aloud, "It is Quasimodo, the cathedral bell-ringer! It is Quasimodo, the hunchback of Notre Dame! Quasimodo, the one-eyed! Quasimodo, the crooked-legged! Hurrah! Hurrah!"

Quasimodo stood at the chapel door, letting himself be admired. A student came up close to him and laughed in his face. Quasimodo merely took him by the belt and cast him with ease ten paces away through the crowd; all without uttering a word.

The noisy guest who had interrupted the play approached Quasimodo.

"By God, you are the most lovely monster that I ever saw in my life! You deserve to be pope of Rome as well as of Paris." The guest laid his hand playfully upon his shoulder. Quasimodo never budged. The guest continued, "Let me entertain you with a Fools' Feast. What do you say?"

Quasimodo made no answer.

"By God," said the guest, "you're not deaf, are you?"

Quasimodo was indeed deaf.

An old woman explained that Quasimodo was deaf, and became so from ringing the bells of Notre Dame. "He talks when he likes," added the woman.

Beggars and thieves along with students and scholars had gone to fetch the paper crown and mock robes of the Pope of Fools. Quasimodo allowed them to put them on him. Then he was seated upon a handcart. Twelve officers of the brotherhood of fools raised the cart to their shoulders; and a sort of bitter, scornful joy dawned upon the sad face of Quasimodo when he saw beneath his feet the heads of so many handsome, straight and well-made men. The howling procession set out, as was the custom, to make the tour of the rooms within the palace before parading the streets and public squares.

Later, when Gringoire, the poor poet and playwright, left the hall, the streets were already dark. He was hungry and cold and went to the Grève, the square where the people had gone to celebrate the Feast of Fools and where he hoped to find a free meal. He hurried to draw near the bonfire that blazed in the middle of the square; but a large crowd formed a circle round about it.

Gringoire discovered that between the crowd and the fire a girl was dancing.

She was not tall, but seemed to be, so proudly straight did she hold her slender figure. She danced, she turned, she twirled, upon an old Persian carpet thrown carelessly beneath her feet; and every time she turned, her great black eyes sent forth lightning flashes.

By the bit of brass that bound her hair, Gringoire understood that she was a Gypsy.

Among the many people watching her, there was one who gazed more closely than all the rest. This man seemed not so old, perhaps thirty-five or so, and yet he was bald; he had but a few gray and sparse locks of hair around his temples. He had dark and passionate deep-set eyes, which he kept fixed on the Gypsy; and while the lively young damsel danced and fluttered to the delight of all, his thoughts seemed to become more and more gloomy.

The girl stopped at last, breathless, and the people applauded eagerly.

"Djali!" said the Gypsy.

A pretty little white goat, with gold-coated horns, gold-coated hooves and a gold-coated collar, walked up to her.

"Djali," said the dancer, "it's your turn now."

And sitting down, she gracefully offered the goat her tambourine. "Djali," she said, "what month in the year is this?"

The goat raised its forefoot and struck once upon the tambourine. It was indeed the first month of the year. The crowd applauded.

"Djali," resumed the girl, turning her tambourine another way, "what day of the month is it?"

Djali lifted his little golden hoof and struck six times upon the tambourine. It was indeed the sixth of January.

"Djali," continued the Gypsy, with still another twist of the tambourine, "what time of day is it?"

Djali gave seven blows, and at the same instant the clock on the Pillar House struck seven.

The people were lost in wonder.

"There is black magic in this," exclaimed a forbidding voice from the crowd. It was the voice of the bald man, who had never taken his eyes from the Gypsy.

"Ah!" said the girl, "it is that ugly man!" Then, pouting, she turned on her heel, and began to collect the gifts of the people in her tambourine. Big pieces of silver, little pieces of silver, pennies and halfpennies rained into it.

Now the crowd made a frenzied rush toward the table of cakes. By the time Gringoire reached the table, there was nothing left to eat.

Just then the parade of the Fools' Pope with its blazing torches and all its music appeared in the Grève. All the actors, vagabonds and thieves of France seemed to be in the mob. In the midst of this throng the high officials of the brotherhood of fools bore upon their shoulders a cart; and upon this cart, clothed in sham royal garb, was the new Fools' Pope, the bell-ringer of Notre Dame, Quasimodo the hunchback.

It is difficult to give any idea of the degree of pride that Quasimodo's hideous and painful face showed during the journey from the palace to the Grève. This was the first thrill of vanity he had ever felt. Before this he had known nothing but humiliation, shame and disgust for himself. Therefore, deaf as he was, he enjoyed the cheering of the mob. His usually gloomy and unhappy face now beamed with joy.

It was surprising, then, at the moment when Quasimodo passed triumphantly before the Pillar House, that the spectators saw a man dart from the crowd and snatch from Quasimodo's hands the staff, the sign of his rank as Fools' Pope.

Upon this cart, clothed in sham royal garb, was the new Fools' Pope, the bell-ringer of Notre Dame, Quasimodo the hunchback.

This man was no other than the bald-headed person who, moments before, had menaced the Gypsy girl. He was now wearing a priest's robes. Just as he stepped forward from the crowd, Gringoire, who had not noticed him till then, recognized him. "Why, it is Claude Frollo, the archdeacon!"

The terrible Quasimodo leapt headlong from his cart, and the women turned away their eyes that they might not see the archdeacon torn limb from limb.

Quasimodo made but one bound toward Claude Frollo, gazed at him and fell on his knees.

The archdeacon tore from Quasimodo his crown, broke his staff and tore his cape.

Quasimodo still knelt, with bowed head and clasped hands.

Then followed between them a strange dialogue in signs and gestures, as neither spoke—the archdeacon standing, angry, threatening, overbearing; Quasimodo, lying down, humble, seeming to ask for forgiveness. And yet it is very certain that Quasimodo could have crushed Claude Frollo with his thumb.

At last the archdeacon, shaking the bell-ringer's powerful shoulder, signed to him to rise and follow. Quasimodo rose.

The brotherhood of fools gathered round to defend their pope. But Quasimodo placed himself before Claude Frollo, flexed his muscles, and glared at the crowd, showing his teeth like an enraged tiger.

They scattered as the archdeacon and Quasimodo vanished down a dark narrow street, where none dared venture after them.

II

The Court of Miracles

"HOW STRANGE!" said Gringoire, but at the rumbling of his empty stomach, his thoughts turned once more to the problem of finding some supper.

Gringoire decided to follow the Gypsy. The townspeople were all going home, and the taverns were closing. The streets grew darker and more deserted every moment. Gringoire had attracted the girl's attention; she had several times turned her head anxiously toward him.

He began to follow at a somewhat greater distance.

But then, at the turn of a street which hid her from his sight, he heard her utter a piercing scream.

He hurried and soon saw the Gypsy struggling in the arms of two men who were trying to stifle her cries. The poor little goat lowered its horns and bleated.

Gringoire rushed boldly forward and one of the two men who held the girl turned toward him. It was Quasimodo.

The hunchback flung Gringoire four paces away upon the pavement and plunged rapidly into the darkness, bearing the girl, thrown over one arm like a silk scarf. His companion followed him, and the poor goat ran behind.

"Murder! murder!" shrieked the Gypsy.

"Halt, wretches, and let that girl go!" exclaimed a horseman who suddenly appeared. It was the captain of the king's archers, armed from head to foot, and sword in hand.

He pulled the girl from the arms of the surprised Quasimodo, laid her across his saddle, and just as the fearless hunchback, recovering from his surprise, rushed upon him to get back his prey, some fifteen or sixteen archers, who were close behind their captain, appeared, swords in hand.

Quasimodo was surrounded, grabbed, tied up. He roared, he foamed at the mouth, he bit; and had it been daylight, no doubt his face alone would have defeated the whole squad. But by night, he was stripped of his most tremendous weapon—his ugliness.

His companion had disappeared during the struggle.

The Gypsy sat gracefully upon the officer's saddle, both hands upon the young man's shoulders, as if charmed by his handsome face and the timely help he had just given her. She said, "What is your name, Mr. Officer?"

"Captain Phoebus de Châteaupers, at your service, my pretty maid!" replied the officer.

"Thank you," said she.

And while Captain Phoebus twirled his moustache, she slipped from the horse and fled.

The captain and his men led away their prisoner, Quasimodo.

Meanwhile, Gringoire, still dizzy from Quasimodo's blow, little by little regained his senses. He discovered he was lying in the gutter. After getting up and walking the streets, without knowing where he was going, Gringoire came to a long narrow lane, which was steep, unpaved and more and more muddy and sloping.

The farther he went down the street, the more thickly did cripples, blind men, and legless men swarm around him, with armless men, one-eyed men, and lepers, some coming out of houses, some from cross streets, howling, yelling, all hobbling and limping, rushing toward the light at the end of the lane.

Gringoire went on, caught up in this stream of men. His fear and dizzy feeling made all of this seem like a horrible dream.

At last he reached the end of the lane. It opened into a vast square, where scattered lights twinkled through the dim fog of night.

"Where am I?" asked Gringoire.

"In the Court of Miracles," replied a figure.

"Miracles?" wondered Gringoire.

"Yes," said the scurrying crippled man. "It's a miracle that I, a cripple all day long, can now run, and that my friend here, Grandfather Carbotte, who is blind during the day, can see now as well as you or I. All of us seem to return to health when we enter these alleys."

The Court of Miracles, Gringoire discovered, was a city of thieves, where beggars by day were transformed into robbers by night.

Gringoire was caught by three beggars and was more and more frightened. A cry rose from the buzzing mob that surrounded him: "Take him to the king! take him to the king!"

They brought him inside a small tavern.

A barrel stood near the fire, and a beggar sat on it. This was the king upon his throne.

The king said, "Who is this rascal? Your name, rascal, and nothing more. Hark ye. You stand before three mighty leaders: me, Clopin Trouillefou, King of the Beggars and Thieves; Mathias Hungadi Spicali, Duke of the Gypsies; Guillaume Rousseau, Emperor of the Gamblers. We are your judges. You have entered our kingdom, the land of thieves, without being a member of the brotherhood. You must be punished, unless you be either thief, beggar or tramp. Are you anything of the sort?"

"Alas," said Gringoire, "I am an author—"

"Enough," cried Trouillefou. "You must be hanged!"

"Noble emperors and kings," said Gringoire, "you do not consider what you're doing. My name is Pierre Gringoire; I am the poet whose play was performed this morning in the Great Hall of the Palace."

"Oh," said Trouillefou. "I was there! Well, friend, because you bored us this afternoon, is that any reason why we should not hang you tonight? But, after all, we wish you no harm. There is one way of getting out of this difficulty. Will you join us?"

"I will indeed, with all my heart," said Gringoire.

"Do you agree to acknowledge yourself a member of the rogues' brigade?"

"Yes."

"A vagabond?"

"Yes."

"To be received by our kingdom, you must prove that you are good for something; and to prove this, you must pickpocket the dummy."

A number of thieves immediately brought out a couple of posts that formed a handy portable gallows. The vagrants then hung a sort of scarecrow from the gallows rope. The scarecrow was so loaded with little bells that they jingled for some time with the swaying of the rope.

Then, the king, showing Gringoire a rickety old footstool, placed it under the dummy and said, "Climb up there!"

"What!" said Gringoire. "I shall break my neck."

The king repeated his order and Gringoire mounted the stool.

"Now," resumed the king, "twist your right foot round your left leg, and stand on tiptoe with your left foot. In that position you can reach the dummy's pockets; you are to search them; you are to take out a purse that you will find there; and if you do all this without ringing a single bell, you shall become a vagabond."

"And if I ring the bells?" asked Gringoire.

"Then you shall be hanged. If I hear but one tinkle, you shall take the dummy's place."

The company of thieves applauded the king's words, and arranged themselves in a ring around the gallows, with pitiless laughter.

Gringoire twisted his right foot round his left leg, stood tiptoe on his left foot, and stretched out his arm, but just as he touched the dummy, his body, now resting on one foot, tottered forward upon the stool; he lost his balance, grabbed at the dummy, and fell heavily to the ground, stunned by the fatal sound of the many tinkling bells he had set off.

The vagabonds laughed.

The voice of the king said, "Lift up the rascal and hang him."

They took down the dummy to make room for Gringoire. The king stepped up to him, passed the rope round his neck, and clapping him on the shoulder, said, "Farewell, mate."

But then he paused. "One moment," he said to Gringoire. "I forgot! It is our custom never to hang a man without asking if there be any woman who'll have him. It's your last chance. You must marry a tramp or the rope." The king remounted his barrel and cried out, "Hello, there, women, females! Is there among you a wench who'll take this scurvy rascal? A man for nothing! Who'll take him?"

Three vagabond women stepped from the crowd to look him over. But none would have him.

"Friend," said the king to Gringoire, "you're down on your luck." Then, standing up on his barrel, he cried, "Will no one take this man? Will no one take him? Going, going, going!" and turning to the gallows, "Gone!"

At this instant a shout rose from the thieves: "Esmeralda!"

The crowd opened and made way for the Gypsy girl!

"Esmeralda!" said Gringoire, astounded.

She approached the victim with her light step. Her pretty goat followed her. She gazed at Gringoire in silence.

"I'll take him," she said.

The Duke of the Gypsies now came forward bringing a jug. The Gypsy girl offered it to Gringoire. "Throw it down," she said to him. For this was the Gypsy wedding ceremony.

The jug broke in four pieces.

"Brother," said the Duke of the Gypsies, laying his hands on their heads, "she is your wife; sister, he is your husband. For four years. Go!"

A few moments later Gringoire found himself in a small room with Esmeralda. There the girl explained to him that she had only married him to save him from hanging, and that she wanted nothing more to do with him.

"Then you don't want me for your husband?" asked Gringoire.

She pouted and answered, "No."

He asked her many more questions about herself, before finally she remarked, "I don't even know your name."

"Pierre Gringoire," said the playwright.

"I know a nicer one," said she.

"Yes?"

"Phoebus," she said. "What does that mean?"

Gringoire answered, "It is a Latin word meaning 'sun.' It is the name of a certain handsome archer who was a god."

"A god!" repeated the Gypsy.

A moment later, the girl and the goat had disappeared, and Gringoire was left alone.

III

Quasimodo's History

SOME SIXTEEN YEARS before the date of this story, on a fine morning of the first Sunday after Easter, known in France as Quasimodo Sunday, a living creature was laid, after Mass, in the Church of Notre Dame, upon a bedstead fixed in the square outside. Upon this bed it was customary to leave unwanted children or orphans to public charity. Whoever chose to take them, did so. In front of the bedstead was a copper basin for alms.

The sort of living creature lying on the board this Sunday morning seemed to excite the curiosity of a numerous group of people, almost all old women.

"What is the world coming to," said one, "if that is the way the children look nowadays?"

"I don't know much about children," said another, "but it must surely be a sin to look at this thing."

"It's no child, it's a deformed monkey."

"I'm sure I hope," exclaimed one, "that no one will offer to take it."

This was no newborn baby. He was a very bony and very uneasy little bundle, tied up in a linen bag, with his head sticking out from one end. This head was a most misshapen thing; there was nothing but a shock of red hair, an eye, a mouth and teeth. The eye wept, the mouth

16

shrieked, and the teeth seemed only waiting for a chance to bite.

Claude Frollo was returning from saying the Mass on Quasimodo Sunday when he noticed the group of old women chattering round the bed for foundlings.

He approached the unfortunate little being who seemed to be so much hated and so much threatened. Its distress and its desertion rushed into his heart at once. He silently went through the crowd, examined the child, and stretched his hand over him. "I adopt this child," said the priest. He wrapped it in his robe and bore it away. The spectators looked at him with frightened eyes.

When he took the child from the sack, he found it terribly deformed indeed. The poor little imp had a wart over his right eye, his head was buried between his shoulders, his spine was curved, his breastbone sticking out, his legs crooked; but he seemed lively. Claude's pity increased at the sight of so much ugliness; and he vowed that he would educate him.

He baptized his adopted child, and named him Quasimodo.

Now, in 1482, Quasimodo had grown up. He had been made, some years previous, bell-ringer of Notre Dame, thanks to Claude Frollo, who had become archdeacon.

In time, a strange bond grew up between the bell-ringer and the church. Notre Dame had been to him by turns, as he grew and developed, egg, nest, home, country, universe. He was as attached to the old church as the tortoise to its shell.

The first time that he grasped the bell-rope in the tower, and clung to it, and set the bell ringing, he seemed to Claude like a child who is beginning to talk.

Quasimodo was born blind in one eye, hunchbacked, lame. It was only by great patience and great painstaking that the priest had succeeded in teaching him to speak. But as bell-ringer of Notre Dame at the age of fourteen, a new disability put the finishing touch to his bad luck; the bells had broken his eardrums. He became deaf.

This deafness shut off his hearing, the only ray of joy and light which reached Quasimodo's soul. That he might not be laughed at, from the moment he realized his deafness he decided not to speak except when alone. When necessity made him talk, his tongue was stiff and awkward, like a door whose hinges have rusted.

The outside world seemed much farther away from him than it does from us. As he grew up, he found nothing but hate. He in turn adopted the weapon—hatred—with which he had been wounded.

His cathedral was enough for him. It was peopled with marble statues of kings, saints and bishops, who at least did not laugh at him and never looked upon him otherwise than with peace and good will. Thus he had long conversations with them. He would sometimes pass whole hours squatting before one of these statues, in a chat with it.

But that which he loved more than all else in the motherly building, that which awakened his soul, that which sometimes actually made him happy was the bells. He loved them, he petted them, he talked to them, he understood them. Yet it was these very bells that made him deaf. But mothers often love that child which has cost them most pain.

To be sure, the voice of the bells was the only one he could still hear. For this reason the big bell was his best beloved. This big bell he had named Marie.

It is impossible to give any idea of his joy on those days when all the bells were rung. When the archdeacon gave him his orders and dismissed him with the word "Go," he ran up the winding staircase more rapidly than anyone else could have gone down.

He called to his assistants, stationed on a lower story of the tower, to begin. They then hung upon the ropes, and the enormous mass of metal moved slowly. Quasimodo, panting with excitement, followed it with his eye. The first stroke of the clapper upon its bronze wall made the wood-beam on which he stood quiver. Quasimodo vibrated with the bell. "Here we go! There we go!" he shouted with a mad burst of laughter.

At last the full peal of bells began; the whole tower shook. Then Quasimodo's joy knew no bounds; he placed himself before the bells. That was the only sound that broke the silence around him. He basked in it as a bird in the sunshine. And then, all at once he flung himself upon the swinging bell. He grasped the bronze monster, clasped it with his knees, spurred it with his heels. As the tower shook, he shouted and gritted his teeth, his red hair standing on end, his chest heaving, his eye flashing fire. As Quasimodo rode the big bell, they became one—half man, half bell.

There was, however, one human being whom Quasimodo excepted from his hatred of mankind in general, and whom he loved as much, perhaps more, than his cathedral—this was Claude Frollo.

That was very natural. The priest had taken him, adopted him, fed him, brought him up. Claude taught him to speak, to read and to write. The priest even made him bell-ringer. Quasimodo's gratitude was boundless. When the poor bell-ringer became deaf, the two worked out a language of

All at once he flung himself upon the swinging bell.

signs. Thus the archdeacon was the only human being with whom Quasimodo kept up any communication. He had relations with but two things in the world—Notre Dame and Claude Frollo.

In 1482 Quasimodo was about twenty years old, the archdeacon about thirty-six. The one had grown up, the other had grown old.

Claude Frollo was now a gloomy, unhappy priest. He had also tried to educate his younger brother. But Jehan Frollo had not grown up in the path in which Claude would have liked to have led him. The big brother expected him to be a devout, studious pupil. But Jehan only grew in the direction of idleness, ignorance and wickedness.

IV
Quasimodo's Punishment

THE DAY AFTER the Feast of Fools, January 7, 1482, a Paris judge woke up in a very sulky and mean mood. He went to the Palace of Justice and sentenced poor Quasimodo (who had been arrested, you remember, by Captain Phoebus) to be whipped in the Grève square, just across the bridge from Notre Dame, and then locked into the pillory by his neck and hands for two hours.

In this square on the right bank, there had already collected a large portion of the population in the hope of witnessing some punishment.

In the ground floor of a tower at one corner of the square was a narrow, arched window guarded by two iron bars placed crosswise, and that looked out upon the square; this window was the only opening through which a little air and light reached the tiny cell without a door. People gave this dark, damp, gloomy cavern the name of the Rat-Hole.

This cell in the Tour-Roland was occupied by Sister Gudule. In 1466, sixteen years earlier to the very month, Paquette la Chantefleurie, as Sister Gudule was then known, gave birth to a little girl. Great was her joy; she had long wished for a child. Her mother was dead, and so Paquette had no one left to love, no one to love her. She prayed night and day that God would give her a child. God had pity on her, and gave her a little girl. I cannot describe to you her delight; she covered the baby with a perfect rain of kisses and caresses. She herself grew pretty again.

It is certain that the child, little Agnes, was dressed up with more ribbons and embroidery than a princess! Among other things, she had a pair of tiny shoes, the like of which even King Louis XI himself surely never had. Her mother sewed and embroidered them herself.

There one day came to the town of Rheims, where Paquette lived, some strange looking men on horseback. They were beggars and vagabonds roaming about the country, under the lead of their duke. They had silver rings in their ears. They came to Rheims to tell fortunes. They looked in your hand and told you the most marvelous things. And yet there were reports of their having stolen children and stolen purses. Wise folks said to the foolish, "Keep away from the Gypsies!"

But poor Paquette was taken with curiosity; she longed to know her child's fortune. So she carried little Agnes to the Gypsies, and they admired the child, caressed her and kissed her, to the great delight of her mother. The child was not a year old then. The next day, Paquette went out, while Agnes was sleeping, to tell a neighbor about her visit to the Gypsies. On her return moments later, she found the door much wider open than she had left it; she went in, poor mother! and ran to the bed. The child was gone; the place was empty. She rushed from the room, flew down the stairs and began to beat the walls with her head, crying, "My child! my child! Who has taken away my child?" The street was deserted, and no one could give her any information. She went through the town, searched every street, ran up and down all day long, mad, out of her senses, like a wild beast that has lost its young.

It was heartbreaking. Poor mother! When night came, she went home. During her absence, a neighbor had seen two Gypsy women go upstairs with a bundle in their arms, then shut the door again and hurry away. After they had gone, a child's cries were heard, coming from Paquette's room. The mother laughed wildly, flew over the stairs as if she had wings, burst open the door and went in. A frightful thing had happened! Instead of her lovely little Agnes, so rosy and fresh, who was a gift from the good God, there lay a hideous little monster, half-blind, lame, deformed, squalling and crawling about the brick floor. He seemed about four years old. The little boy, of course, was quickly removed; he would have driven her mad.

Paquette flung herself upon the little shoe—all that was left of all that she had loved. Suddenly she got up and ran to the Gypsy camp. They were all gone. The next day, several miles away, on a heath were found the remains of a great fire, some ribbons which had belonged to Paquette's child, drops of blood and some goat hair. No one doubted that the Gypsies had killed the child. When Paquette heard these horrible things, she did not shed a tear; but the next day her hair was gray. On the following day she disappeared.

Some time later she reappeared in Paris, as the nun Sister Gudule, and entered the cell in the Tour-Roland.

The Gypsy child was of course the same one claimed as a foundling by Claude Frollo—Quasimodo.

Poor Quasimodo was about to be led onto this square (where Sister Gudule lived holed up in Tour-Roland) to be whipped!

Meanwhile, there was still that crowd gathered in the square by the pillory, where public punishments took place. A very steep flight of stairs led to the upper platform, upon which was a wheel made of oak. The victim would be bound to this wheel in a kneeling position, with his hands behind him. The wheel would revolve, presenting the prisoner's face to each side of the square.

When the victim appeared, and was led to the wheel, the spectators recognized Quasimodo.

Quasimodo was tied with chains and leather ropes. He was placed upon his knees on the wheel; he made no fight. He was stripped of his shirt to the waist. A shout of laughter ran through the crowd when Quasimodo's hump, his camel breast, his hairy shoulders were bared to view. During this burst of merriment, a man in city uniform mounted the platform and took his place by the prisoner's side. He was the official torturer.

He stamped his foot and the wheel began to turn. Quasimodo was suddenly astonished and the spectators laughed.

The torturer began his work with his whip; the thin lashes hissed through the air like a brood of vipers, and fell furiously upon the wretched man's shoulders.

Quasimodo writhed in his bonds; surprise and pain distorted the muscles of his face, but he did not heave a sigh. He merely bent his head back, to the right, then to the left.

A second blow followed the first, then a third, and another, and another, and so on and so on. Quasimodo closed his single eye, dropped his head upon his breast, and seemed dead.

At the end of an hour, the torture stopped. Quasimodo's eye reopened slowly. Two attendants of the torturer washed the victim's bleeding shoulders, rubbed them with some salve, which at once closed all the wounds, and threw over Quasimodo's back a piece of cotton cloth.

But all was not over for Quasimodo. He had still to spend two hours on that pillory.

Countless insults rained upon him, mingled with hoots, curses, laughter and occasional stones. Jehan Frollo, Claude's own brother, mocked the poor hunchback: "You deserve to hang, you devil!"

The wretched man, unable to break the collar that held him chained like a wild beast, heaved a sigh. Then, for a moment, as a mule passed through the crowd, bearing a priest on its back, Quasimodo's face, previously full of rage, hate and despair, softened. As the priest approached, Quasimodo smiled! Yet the priest cast down his eyes, turned back suddenly and hurried away, not wanting to be greeted and recognized by the poor man.

The priest was the archdeacon Claude Frollo.

Quasimodo's face grew dark.

Time passed. Suddenly he again struggled in his chains and broke his silence, crying in a hoarse and furious voice, "Water!"

This cry of distress, instead of making the people feel sorry for him, made them mock at him even more.

In a few minutes Quasimodo repeated, "Water!"

Everyone laughed.

"Drink that!" shouted a cruel friend of Jehan Frollo, flinging in Quasimodo's face a sponge that had been dragged through the gutter. "There, you deaf monster!"

A woman aimed a stone at his head, saying, "That will teach you to wake us at night with your cursed bell-ringing!"

"Water!" repeated the gasping Quasimodo for the third time.

At this moment he saw the crowd separate. A girl, oddly dressed, stepped from their midst. She was accompanied by a little white goat with gilded horns, and held a tambourine in her hand.

Quasimodo's eye gleamed. It was the Gypsy! He did not doubt that she too came to be avenged, and to torment and tease him with the rest.

He watched her climb the ladder. Rage and spite choked him. He longed to destroy the pillory and the girl.

Without a word Esmeralda approached the sufferer, who tried to twist to avoid her, and, unfastening a gourd of water from her belt, she raised it gently to the parched lips of the miserable man.

Then from that eye, so dry and burning, a great tear trickled, and rolled slowly down the misshapen face. It was perhaps the first tear Quasimodo had ever shed.

But he forgot to drink. The Gypsy made a pout of impatience, and then smilingly pressed the neck of the gourd to Quasimodo's mouth.

He drank long and deep; his thirst was desperate.

When he had done, the poor wretch put out his lips to kiss the fair hand that had helped him. But the girl, remembering his attempt to kidnap her the previous night, pulled away her hand.

Then the poor deaf man fixed upon her a look of sadness for not trusting him.

The people watching this sad, beautiful scene began to clap their hands and shout, "Hurrah! Hurrah!"

It was at this moment that Sister Gudule saw, from the window of her cell, the Gypsy girl upon the pillory, and shouted, "May you be cursed, Gypsy! Cursed! Cursed!"

Esmeralda turned pale and climbed down the pillory and fled.

The hour had now come to release Quasimodo, and the mob left the square.

V

Esmeralda in Danger

SEVERAL WEEKS had passed.

One day as the sun was sinking toward the west,
Esmeralda was dancing in the square before Notre Dame.

A priest, meanwhile, at the top of one of the towers of
Notre Dame, was leaning on his elbows. This was, of
course, archdeacon Claude Frollo, absorbed in one sight,
one thought. All Paris lay beneath his feet, with its countless steeples and gentle hills, with its river winding beneath its bridges, and its people flowing through its streets,
with its cloud of smoke and its chain of roofs crowding
Notre Dame; but of the whole city, the archdeacon saw
only one corner—the square in front of the cathedral; only
one figure in all that crowd—the Gypsy.

The Gypsy danced; she twirled her tambourine upon the
tip of her finger and tossed it into the air. The crowd
swarmed around her. Now and then a man dressed in a
red and yellow coat waved the people back into a circle,
then sat down again in a chair a few feet away from the
dancer, and let the goat lay its head upon his knee. This
man seemed to be the Gypsy's friend.

The priest muttered between his teeth, "Who is that
man? I have always seen her alone till now!" He was
jealous!

Then Claude Frollo plunged down the winding stairs. He saw Quasimodo, who was leaning from a window, also gazing out into the square. His savage eye had a strange expression; it looked both charmed and gentle. "How strange," thought the priest. "Can he also be looking at the Gypsy?"

In a few moments Claude Frollo came out into the square through the door at the foot of the tower.

"What has become of the Gypsy girl?" he asked, joining the group of spectators.

"I don't know," answered one. "She just vanished. I think she has gone to dance in the house over there."

In the Gypsy's place, upon the same carpet, the archdeacon saw no one but the red-and-yellow man, who was walking round the ring, his elbows on his hips, his head thrown back, his neck stretched and a chair between his teeth.

"By our lady!" cried the archdeacon, "what is the poet Pierre Gringoire doing here?"

Gringoire was the red-and-yellow man; he was so alarmed by the priest's voice that he lost his balance and fell.

Claude Frollo signaled for the young man to follow him into the church.

"How has it happened that you are now keeping company with that Gypsy dancing-girl?"

Gringoire gave the priest a brief account of his adventure in the Court of Miracles, and his so-called marriage. "My wife is a foundling or a lost child. She wears about her neck an amulet that the Gypsies say will some day restore her to her parents, but which will lose its power should she lose her virtue. But, Archdeacon, what difference does it make to you?"

The priest's cheek turned red. "Because I wish you well. The slightest contact with that devilish Gypsy girl would make you the slave of Satan. You know that it is always the body which destroys the soul. That is all."

Ever since the morning when he was whipped and tied up on the pillory, the people living in the neighborhood of Notre Dame fancied that Quasimodo's zeal for bell-ringing had grown very cold. Up to that time he had pulled the bells upon every occasion and no occasion at all. Now the cathedral seemed sad and silent. It seemed as if there were no musician left in the towers. And yet, Quasimodo was still there. What had happened to him? Had the pain caused by the whipping killed his love for the bells? Or did big Marie—as he called the belfry's largest bell—have a rival in the heart of the ringer of Notre Dame, and were Marie and her fourteen ringing sisters neglected for a fairer and more attractive object?

It happened that today, on the Feast of the Annunciation, the twenty-fifth of March, the air was so pure and so clear that Quasimodo felt some slight return of his love for the bells. He therefore climbed up into the high belfry cage in the north tower, and gazed at the bells there. He set them swinging and felt that cluster of bells vibrating beneath his touch; and he was happy again.

He clapped his hands, he ran from one rope to another, he encouraged the bronze singers, as a conductor spurs on an orchestra.

"Go on," he cried; "go on, Gabrielle! Pour all your music into the public square; this is a high holiday. Go on, Allegra!"

He was urging on the bells, calling them by name, and they bounded to and fro as best they could, and shook their shining sides.

All at once, as his gaze fell beyond the steep belfry wall, he saw in the square the Gypsy girl, surrounded by spectators. This sight suddenly changed the course of his ideas, and chilled his interest in the music. He stopped, turned his back on the chime of the bells, and crouched within the belfry, staring down at the dancing-girl with the dreamy, tender, gentle look that had once before astonished the archdeacon. The bells stopped suddenly, to the great disappointment of the lovers of chimes in the neighborhood below.

One morning, after a visit from his worthless, lazy brother, Claude Frollo secretly followed Jehan, to whom he had lent some money for books. Jehan met up with his friend, none other than Captain Phoebus de Châteaupers. They, with Claude Frollo's money, went out to a tavern to get drunk. On the way there, Claude overheard the officer say to Jehan, "Thunder! We must hurry."

"Why, Phoebus?"

"Tonight I have to see the Gypsy girl, the one with the goat."

"Really?" said Jehan.

"I swear it!"

"Tonight?"

"Tonight."

"Are you sure she will come?"

"There's no doubt, Jehan."

The archdeacon heard every word of this; jealous about the girl he wanted to hate, his teeth chattered; he shook from head to foot. He stood still a moment, then followed in the track of the two scamps.

That night, Claude Frollo was waiting for the young drunkards in front of the noisy tavern they had entered hours before. His cloak was pulled up to his very nose. At last the tavern door opened and the two men came out.

"Thunder and guns!" said Phoebus. "It is the hour of my appointment. Jehan, have we drunk up all the money the priest gave you? Haven't you any left? I need it."

But Jehan was too drunk to answer sensibly, and fell over onto a heap of garbage. Phoebus left him there and went on.

Claude Frollo followed the captain and left his own brother to sleep under the friendly watch of the bright stars.

As Phoebus continued on his way, he discovered that someone was following him. "Sir," he called out, "if you are a robber, you've come to the wrong place."

The shadow in the cloak suddenly stretched out and swooped down upon Phoebus' arm with the grip of an eagle. "Captain Phoebus de Châteaupers?"

"What the devil!" said Phoebus. "Do you know my name?"

"I not only know your name," replied the man in the cloak, "but I know that you have an appointment this evening."

"Yes."

"With a woman?"

"Yes. Her name is Esmeralda."

"Then go to your appointment," said Claude Frollo.

"I shall," said Phoebus, "but I find that I will have no money to pay the innkeeper."

In response to this the man in the cloak slipped some money to Phoebus.

"My goodness," said the captain, "you're a good fellow!"

"I give this on one condition," said the priest. "Prove to me that you spoke the truth. Hide me in some corner where I can see whether this woman be really Esmeralda."

"At your service," said the captain. They then set forth at a fast pace.

On entering a disgusting inn, Phoebus' mysterious friend pulled his cloak up to his eyes. An old woman led them up a ladder. On reaching the upper floor, Phoebus showed the priest a place where he could hide, and then the captain and the old woman went back downstairs.

Claude Frollo settled himself down to wait. He waited a quarter of an hour; all at once he heard the boards of the ladder creak; someone was coming up. There was a considerable hole in the worm-eaten door of his prison; to this he glued his face. He could see everything that happened in the next room. The old woman first rose from the trapdoor, lamp in hand; then came Phoebus; then a third person—Esmeralda. The priest trembled on seeing her. After the old woman left, Phoebus and Esmeralda were alone, seated on the wooden chest below the lamp.

The girl was blushing, shaking and confused. Her long, drooping eyelashes shaded her red cheeks. Her feet were hidden, for the little goat was lying upon them.

"Oh," said the girl, without raising her eyes, "do not despise me, Phoebus! I feel that I am doing very wrong for coming here with you. I am breaking a sacred vow. I shall never find my parents! The amulet will lose its power, and I my virtue; but what does that matter? Why should I need father or mother now?"

So saying, she fixed upon the captain her large dark eyes, moist with love and joy.

"I can't say I understand you!" exclaimed Phoebus.

Esmeralda was silent for a moment, then a tear fell from her eyes, a sigh from her lips, and she said, "Oh, my lord, I love you!"

Phoebus and Esmeralda were alone, seated on the wooden chest below the lamp.

"You love me!" said he; and he threw his arm around the Gypsy's waist.

"Phoebus, you are good, you are generous, you are kind; you saved me—me, who am but a poor Gypsy foundling. I have long dreamed of an officer who should save my life. I love my captain."

"Look here, my dear—"

The Gypsy gave him a few little taps on the lips with her pretty hand. "No, no, I will not listen. I want you to tell me if you love me."

"Do I love you, angel of my life!" cried the captain. "I am all yours—all yours. I love you, and never loved anyone but you."

The captain had so often repeated this phrase to other girls that he uttered it in one breath.

The captain pressed his lips to her shoulders.

Claude Frollo saw all. The priest shuddered and burned at this scene of love, darkness and passion. The young and lovely girl, her clothes in disorder, made him shake.

Suddenly, above the head of Phoebus, Esmeralda saw another head—an angry face with a hand that held a knife. It was the face and hand of the priest; he had broken down the door, and he was there. Phoebus could not see him. The girl was frozen at the sight of this frightful man. She could not even utter a cry. She saw a knife come down upon Phoebus and rise again dripping with blood.

The captain screamed and fell.

Esmeralda fainted.

When she recovered her senses, she was surrounded by soldiers, some of whom were carrying off the captain bathed in his own blood; the priest had vanished; the window at the back of the room, which opened upon the river, was wide open. She heard someone around her say, "She is a witch who has stabbed the captain."

VI

Sanctuary!

GRINGOIRE and the entire Court of Miracles were terribly worried. Esmeralda had not been heard from for a whole long month; nor did anyone know what had become of her goat, which increased Gringoire's grief; for he loved Djali as much as he loved the girl.

One day as Gringoire was walking, he noticed a crowd before one of the doors of the Palace of Justice.

"What's the matter?" he asked a young man who was just coming out.

"I don't know," replied the young man. "I hear that they are having a trial for a woman who murdered an officer. It seems there was witchcraft about it."

The prisoner, it turned out, was Esmeralda.

She was pale; her hair fell about her in disorder; her lips were white; her eyes seemed hollow.

"Phoebus!" she cried out wildly; "where is he? Oh, gentlemen, before you kill me, in pity tell me if he still lives!"

"Be silent, woman!" said the president of the judges; "that does not concern us."

"Oh, have mercy! Tell me if he is alive!" she repeated, clasping her beautiful hands; and her chains rattled as she moved.

The president of the judges called out, "Bring in the other prisoner."

All eyes were turned upon a small door that opened, and to Gringoire's great dismay, a pretty goat, with gilded horns and hoofs, appeared. All at once Djali saw Esmeralda, and leaping over the table and the head of a clerk, she was at the girl's knees; then she curled herself at her feet.

"If it please you, gentlemen," said the prosecutor, "we will proceed to examine the goat."

The prosecutor took from a table the Gypsy girl's tambourine and, presenting it to the goat in a particular way, he asked the creature:

"What time is it?"

The goat looked at him, lifted her gilded hoof and struck seven blows. It was indeed seven o'clock. Those same spectators who had clapped for the innocent tricks of Djali in the public streets were terrified by them within the walls of the Palace of Justice.

It was still worse when, the prosecutor having emptied out upon the floor a certain leather bag full of letters, which Djali wore about her neck, the goat selected with her foot the separate letters spelling out the fatal name "Phoebus." In all eyes, the Gypsy girl—that dancer who had so often dazzled the passers-by—was nothing but a horrible witch.

The president of the judges raised his voice and said, "Girl, you are a Gypsy, a witch. You, with your bewitched goat, did, upon the night of the twenty-ninth of March, murder and stab, together with the powers of darkness, by the aid of charms and spells, a captain of the king's troops, one Phoebus de Châteaupers. Upon such day as it shall please the lord our king, at the hour of noon, you shall be taken in your dress, barefoot, a rope around your neck, to the square before the great door of Notre Dame, and shall there do proper penance; and from there you shall be taken to the Grève, where you shall be hanged on the city gallows; and likewise for your goat. May God have mercy on your soul."

"Oh, it is a dream!" she said; and she was carried off to her cell.

One morning, as the May sun was rising, the grieving nun of the Tour-Roland heard the noise of wheels, and horses' hoofs and the clink of iron in the square outside her cell. She tried not to hear these sounds, and fell to her knees staring at the object that she had adored for fifteen years. This little shoe was the entire universe to her. Her every thought was bound up in it, never to be parted until death.

On this particular morning it seemed as if she were more broken-hearted than usual; and those who passed by outside heard her wailing in a loud tone.

"Oh, my daughter," she moaned, "my daughter! My poor, dear little child, I shall never see you again! It always seems to me as if it were but yesterday that it happened! Alas, alas! here is the shoe, but where is the foot; where is the rest; where is my child?"

The unhappy woman burst into heartbreaking sobs as if it were the very day it happened; for to a mother who has lost her child, her loss is ever present. Such grief as that never grows old.

At this instant the fresh, happy voices of a band of children were heard outside, passing the cell. Usually, every time that a child met her eye or ear, the poor mother rushed into the blackest corner of her hole, and seemed as if she were trying to bury her head in the walls. But today, on the contrary, she sprang up and listened. One of the little boys said, "They are going to hang the Gypsy girl today."

With a sudden leap, the woman ran to her window, which looked, as you recall, upon the square. A ladder was indeed built close to the gallows, and the hangman's assistant was arranging the chains. A number of people stood about watching him.

The laughing group of children had already vanished. The nun looked about for some passer-by, whom she might question. She noticed, close by her cell, a priest. She recognized him as the archdeacon of Notre Dame.

"Father," she asked, "who is to be hanged there? The children said it was a Gypsy girl."

"I believe it is," said Claude Frollo.

Then Sister Gudule burst into a laugh.

"Sister," said the archdeacon, "do you hate the Gypsies so much?"

"Do I hate them!" cried the woman; "they are witches, child-stealers! They took my little girl, my only child! I have no heart now! There is one I hate the most, and whom I have cursed. She is young, about the age that my daughter would have been if her mother had not murdered my girl. Every time that snake passes my cell my blood boils!"

"Well, then, sister, rejoice," said the priest. "It is the same girl whose death you are about to witness."

The recluse was joyous. "I told her she would climb those steps to the gallows! Thanks, sir priest!" she cried.

In spite of the sentence of "murder" pronounced upon poor Esmeralda, Phoebus was not dead. For a week the surgeon and soldiers feared for his life. And then, one fine morning, feeling better, he got up and walked away. The judges did not care about this fact. They believed Phoebus to be dead, and that was the end of it.

Phoebus, in fact, had not gone far, a few stations away from Paris. He had a feeling that he would seem somehow silly in the courts, and so he avoided the case. He did not worry about Esmeralda; he had no idea whether it was the Gypsy or the mysterious man who had stabbed him.

Feeling sure that after two months the Gypsy trial must be past and forgotten, he returned to Paris. He paid no attention to a somewhat numerous crowd that had gathered in the square in front of Notre Dame. He went into a house on the square to see an attractive young woman.

He and this woman went out onto the balcony of her house.

A vast number of people overflowed the square of Notre Dame into all the nearby streets. The entrance of the cathedral was guarded by the bishop's armed soldiers. The wide church doors were closed.

Esmeralda would be lectured here in the square by a priest, be told to ask for forgiveness, and then be sent over the bridge to the Grève square to be hanged.

The clock of Notre Dame slowly struck twelve. The crowd murmured with satisfaction.

"There she is!"

A wagon, drawn by a strong horse, and entirely surrounded by cavalry wearing purple with white crosses, had just entered the square. Officers of the watch made a passage for it through the people. Beside the wagon rode a number of officers of justice and of police. The official torturer walked in front of them. In the fatal wagon sat a girl, her arms bound behind her. She was in her flimsy short dress; her long black curls fell upon her chest and over her shoulders.

She had a rough, gray rope about her neck. At her feet was the little goat, also tied with a rope.

The captain, recognizing her, did not want her to see him.

The parade of the wagon and its attendants had made its way through the crowd. Many people, even the meanest, were touched with pity at the sight of Esmeralda—so much beauty and so much misery.

The wagon stopped in front of the central doors of Notre Dame. The mob was hushed; the great doors moved upon their creaky hinges. Then the entire length of the deep, dark church was seen. Priests were chanting a mass for the dead.

The people listened quietly.

The victim, in her terror, seemed to lose all power of sight and thought. Her lips moved as if in prayer.

The hangman's assistant went to her and untied her hands. She got down from the cart with her goat, which was also untied, and which bleated with delight at regaining its freedom. Esmeralda was then led barefooted over the hard pavement to the foot of the steps leading to the church porch. The rope about her neck trailed behind her.

Then the chanting in the church stopped. A few moments later a long line of priests marched toward the prisoner, singing psalms as they came. Esmeralda's eyes were fixed upon the one who walked in front.

"Oh," she whispered to herself with a shudder, "there he is again!—the priest!"

It was indeed the archdeacon Claude Frollo.

When he appeared in full daylight under the arch of the doorway, he was pale, like a statue.

She, no less pale and no less like a statue, hardly noticed that a lighted candle had been placed in her hand;

she did not hear the voice of the clerk reading the fatal lines of the words with which she was to ask forgiveness; when she was told to answer "Amen," she answered "Amen." When she saw the priest signal to her jailers to move away, and he approached her, then she was in a fury.

He said to her aloud, "Girl, have you asked God to pardon your sins?"

He bent to her ear and whispered: "Will you be mine? I can still save you!"

"What have you done with my Phoebus?"

"He is dead!" said the priest.

At this moment, Claude Frollo raised his head and saw at the opposite end of the square, upon the balcony of a house, Captain Phoebus himself standing beside a young woman! The archdeacon staggered, passed his hand over his eyes, looked again, murmured a curse and made a terrible face.

"So be it!" Claude Frollo said to Esmeralda. "Die! No one else shall have you if I cannot."

Then, raising his hand above the Gypsy girl's head, he told the executioner that the ceremonies were over, and that the girl now belonged to the hangman.

He turned his back upon the prisoner, rejoined the parade of priests, and a moment later disappeared beneath the dim arches of the cathedral.

The prisoner stood in her place, awaiting her doom. The hangman's assistants approached the girl and retied her hands.

The unhappy Esmeralda, as she was about to remount the fatal wagon and advance on her last journey, raised her eyes to heaven, to the sun, to the clouds here and there in the blue sky; then she looked at the ground, at the crowd, at the houses. Suddenly, while the men were tying her arms, she shrieked—a shriek of joy. Upon the balcony of the house at the corner of the square, she now had just seen him, her love, her Phoebus—alive!

The judge had lied! The priest had lied! It was he, she knew it; he was there, handsome, living, dressed in his fancy uniform.

"Phoebus!" she cried. "My Phoebus!"

And she tried to stretch out her arms, but they were tied up.

Then she saw the captain frown, and a lovely young woman next to him looked at him with angry eyes; then Phoebus spoke a few words Esmeralda could not hear, and both persons vanished through the balcony window, which closed behind them.

Esmeralda fell to the ground.

"Come," said the hangman, "lift her into the wagon and let us make an end of this!"

No one had seen, in the row of statues of kings carved just above the arches of the church porch, a strange spectator.

Just as the hangman's assistants were about to lift up Esmeralda, this strange man slid down a rope, as a drop of rain glides down a window, rushed toward the two men, knocked them to the ground with his two huge fists, picked up the Gypsy girl in one hand, as a child might pick up a doll, and with one leap was in the church, holding her above his head, and shouting in a tremendous voice, "Sanctuary!"

"Sanctuary! Sanctuary!" repeated the mob; and as the thousands of spectators applauded, Quasimodo was proud and pleased.

This shock brought Esmeralda to her senses. She raised

her eyelids, looked at Quasimodo, then closed them suddenly.

The hangman and all his men stood astounded. It was true; within Notre Dame, the prisoner was safe; the cathedral was a sure place of refuge; the law of France could not come in.

Quasimodo had paused beneath the great doorway. His big bushy head was buried between his shoulders like the head of a lion with a mane. He held the girl, who was trembling from head to foot, in his huge hands; but he carried her as carefully as if he was afraid he should break or injure her. He seemed to feel that she was a precious thing. Then, suddenly, he pulled her close in his arms, upon his misshapen chest, as his treasure, as his only wealth, as her mother might have done. His eye flashed love. Then the women in the mob outside laughed and wept, the men stamped their feet in approval and admiration, for at that instant Quasimodo was truly beautiful. He was beautiful—he, that orphan, that foundling, that outcast.

How touching was the protection given by so deformed a creature to one so unfortunate as the girl condemned to die, and saved by Quasimodo!

However, after a few moments of triumph, Quasimodo hurried into the church. The crowd on the square, admiring his strength, followed him with their eyes. All at once he reappeared at one end of the long row of statues of kings; he ran along like a madman, holding his prize in the air, and shouting "Sanctuary!" The crowd broke into fresh applause. He again rushed within the church. A moment later, he reappeared upon the upper platform, the Gypsy still in his arms, still running, still shouting, "Sanctuary!" and the mob applauded. At last he appeared

At last he appeared for the third time upon the tower of the big bell; from there he seemed proud to show the whole city the girl he had saved.

for the third time upon the top of the tower of the big bell; from there he seemed proud to show the whole city the girl he had saved, and his thundering voice—that voice so rarely heard by anyone, and never by himself—repeated three times, "Sanctuary! Sanctuary! Sanctuary!"

"Hurrah! Hurrah!" cried the people in response; and their vast shout was heard with amazement by the people in the square of the Grève, and by the cell-bound woman, who still waited, her eyes on the hangman's gallows.

VII

Living in the Cathedral

EVERY CITY in the Middle Ages had its places of refuge, its sanctuaries. Having once set foot within the sanctuary, the criminal was sacred; but let him beware if he tried to leave; one step outside his shelter and guards would take him. It sometimes happened that a ruling from Parliament violated the sanctuary, and gave up the criminal to justice; but this was rare.

Churches usually had a cell prepared to receive those seeking refuge. At Notre Dame it was a cell built over the aisles. It was here that Quasimodo had placed Esmeralda after his race through the towers and galleries. While that race lasted, the girl did not recover her senses—half dozing, half waking, knowing only that she was being carried through the air. From time to time she heard the noisy laughter, the rough voice of Quasimodo in her ear. She half opened her eyes; then beneath her she saw all Paris dotted with countless roofs; above her head the fearful grinning face of Quasimodo. Her eyelids fell; she thought that all was over, that she had been hanged, and that this strange spirit had carried her away.

But when the bell-ringer had set her down in the cell of refuge, when she felt his huge hands gently untie the rope that hurt her arms, she awoke and saw that she was still in

47

Notre Dame; she remembered being pulled from the hangman's hands; that Phoebus lived, that Phoebus had stopped loving her. She turned to Quasimodo, who stood before her, and said, "Why did you save me?"

He looked at her, trying to guess what she said. He turned and ran away.

A few moments later he returned, bringing a bundle, which he threw at her feet. It contained clothes left at the door of the church for her by kind women.

Quasimodo covered his eye and again left.

When Quasimodo returned he carried a basket under one arm and a mattress under the other. In the basket were a bottle, a loaf of bread and some other food. He set the basket down and said, "Eat!" He spread the mattress on the floor and said, "Sleep!"

It was his own food, his own bed, which the bell-ringer had brought.

The Gypsy lifted her eyes to his face to thank him, but she could not speak. The poor man was hideous indeed. She shuddered with fright.

Then he said, "I scare you. I am very ugly, am I not? Do not look at me; only listen to me. During the day you must stay here; by night, you can walk anywhere about the church; but do not leave the church by day or night. They would kill you, and I should die."

Moved by his words, she raised her head to reply. He had vanished. Alone once more, she thought about the words of this almost monstrous man, struck by the sound of his voice, which was so hoarse and yet so gentle.

Then she looked around at her cell. It was a room with a little window and a door opening onto a slightly sloping roof. Beyond the roof she saw the tops of a thousand chimneys, from which poured out the smoke of all the fires of Paris. This was a sad sight for the poor Gypsy girl—a foundling, condemned to death, unhappy, without a country, without a family, without a home.

Just then she felt a hairy, bearded head rub against her hands and knees. She trembled (everything frightened her now) and looked down. It was the poor goat, the nimble Djali, who had escaped with her when Quasimodo rescued her, and who had been at her feet for nearly an hour without earning a glance. The Gypsy girl covered the goat with kisses.

"Oh, Djali!" said she, "how could I forget you! But you never forget me! Oh, you at least are not ungrateful."

She began to weep; and as her tears flowed, she felt the sharpest and bitterest of her grief going from her with them.

When evening came, she thought the night so beautiful, the moon so soft, that she took a walk in the raised gallery that runs around the church. She felt somewhat refreshed by it, the earth seemed to her so peaceful, viewed from that height.

The next morning, she found, on waking, the unhappy face of Quasimodo at the window. She closed her eyes. Then she heard his rough voice saying very kindly, "Don't be scared. I am your friend. I came to see if you were asleep. It does you no harm, does it, if I look at you when you are asleep? What does it matter to you if I am here when your eyes are shut? Now I will go. There, I have hidden myself behind the wall. You can open your eyes again."

The Gypsy girl opened her eyes. He was no longer at the window. She went to the window and saw that the poor hunchback was crouched in a corner by the wall. "Come here," she said gently. From the motion of her lips, Quasimodo thought she was ordering him to go away; he therefore got up and limped slowly away, with his head hanging, not daring to raise his eye to the girl's face.

"Come here!" she cried. But he still went on. Then she ran out of her cell, hurried after him, and took his arm. When he felt her touch, Quasimodo trembled in every limb. He raised his sad eye and, finding that she drew him toward her, his whole face beamed with tenderness and delight. She tried to make him enter her cell; but he remained in the doorway. "No, no," said he; "the owl must not enter the lark's nest."

For some moments both Quasimodo and Esmeralda were motionless, gazing at each other—he, at so much beauty; she, at so much ugliness. Her gaze went from his knock-knees to his hunchback, from his back to his single eye.

He was the first to break the silence: "Did you tell me to come back?"

She nodded her head as she said, "Yes."

He understood her nod. "Alas!" said he, "I am—I am deaf."

"Poor man!" cried the Gypsy.

He smiled sadly.

"Yes, I am deaf. It is horrible, isn't it? And you—you are so beautiful! I never realized my ugliness until now. When I compare myself with you, I pity myself indeed, poor unhappy monster that I am. I must seem to you like some awful beast, eh? You—you are a sunbeam, a bird's song! As for me, I am something frightful, neither man nor beast, more hard, shapeless and stepped upon than a pebble."

Then he began to laugh, and that laugh was heart-breaking. "Yes, I am deaf; but you can speak to me by gestures, by signs. I have a master who talks with me in that way. And then I shall know your wishes from the motion of your lips, and your expression."

"Well," she replied, smiling, "tell me why you saved me."

He watched her closely as she spoke.

"I understand you," he said. "You ask me why I saved you. You have forgotten a villain who tried to carry you off one night—a villain to whom the very next day you brought relief upon the terrible pillory. A drink of water and a little pity are more than my whole life can ever repay. You have forgotten that villain; but he remembers."

She listened with deep feeling.

Then he turned to go away.

She signed to him to stay.

"No, no," said he, "I must not stay too long. I am not at my ease. It is out of pity that you do not turn away your eyes. I will go where I can see you without your seeing me. That will be better."

He drew from his pocket a small metal whistle.

"There," he said, "when you need me, when you wish me to come to you, when I do not horrify you too much, whistle with this. I hear that sound."

He laid the whistle on the ground, and fled.

One day followed another. Each day's rising found Esmeralda breathing better, less pale. Her grace and beauty bloomed again.

The Gypsy sometimes thought of Quasimodo. He was the only connection with mankind left to her. She could not understand the strange friend whom chance had given her. She often scolded herself for not feeling enough thankfulness to be able to blind herself to his terrible ugliness.

Once Quasimodo appeared just as she was petting Djali. He stood for a few moments looking at the pretty girl and goat; at last he said, shaking his heavy, clumsy head, "My bad luck is that I am still too much like a human being. I wish I were completely an animal like that goat."

One morning Esmeralda went out to the edge of the roof and looked into the square. Quasimodo stood behind her. Seeing something, she became startled. She knelt on the edge of the roof and stretched out her arms, crying, "Phoebus! Come to me!"

Quasimodo bent over the edge and saw that she was calling to a young man, a captain, a handsome knight, who pranced through the square on horseback. However, the officer did not hear the girl's call; he was too far away.

Quasimodo muttered, "Oh, so that is how a man should look! He only needs a handsome outside!"

Meanwhile, Esmeralda was on her knees, crying, "Phoebus! Phoebus!"

The deaf man watched her. He understood her. His eyes filled with tears. Then he plucked Esmeralda gently by the hem of her sleeve. She turned. He said, "Shall I go and fetch him?"

She uttered a cry of joy.

"Oh, go! go! run, quick! Bring him to me! I will love you!"

"I will bring him to you," said Quasimodo. Then he turned his head and hurried quickly down the stairs, sobbing.

When he reached the square, he saw nothing but the fine horse tied to a post at the door of a house; the captain had already entered. Quasimodo raised his eyes to the roof of the church. Esmeralda was still in the same place, in the same position. Quasimodo leaned against one of the posts in front of the house and waited for the captain.

The whole day passed like this. At last night came, and finally Phoebus left the house.

The bell-ringer let him turn the corner of the street, then ran after him, shouting, "Hello, there, Captain!"

Phoebus stopped.

"Follow me, Captain; there is someone who wishes to speak with you."

The captain started away.

Quasimodo cried, "Come, Captain, it is a woman who loves you."

"You beast!" said Phoebus. "Do you think I have to go to all the women who love me, or say they do? How do I know she doesn't look like you? Tell the woman who sent you that I am about to marry, and that she may go to the devil!"

"Hear me," said Quasimodo. "It is the Gypsy girl!"

"The Gypsy girl!" he exclaimed, almost terrified, for he did not know of her amazing rescue and thought she had been hanged. "Do you come from the world of the dead?"

"Quick, quick!" said the deaf man, "this way."

Phoebus gave Quasimodo a quick kick. "Go away!" said the captain, who then rode off on his horse.

Quasimodo returned to Notre Dame and climbed the tower. The Gypsy was waiting along the roof edge.

"Alone!" she cried, seeing him.

"I could not find him," lied the hunchback.

"You should have waited all night," she replied angrily.

He saw her gesture and understood her scolding.

"I will watch better another time," said he, hanging his head.

"Go away!" she said.

He left her. She was offended with him. But he would rather be maltreated by her than make her unhappy with the truth about the captain.

From that day on, the Gypsy did not see Quasimodo any

more. He stopped visiting her cell. At most, she sometimes caught a glimpse of the bell-ringer on top of a tower, gazing sadly at her. But as soon as she saw him, he disappeared.

As usual, however, her food appeared while she slept. One morning she found a cage of birds on her windowsill. She passed her days in petting Djali, in watching the square, in talking to herself about Phoebus and in feeding the birds.

She had stopped seeing or hearing Quasimodo at all; the poor hunchback seemed to have vanished. But one night, when she could not sleep, and was thinking of her handsome captain, she heard a sigh close by her cell. Terrified, she got up, and saw by the light of the moon a heap lying outside across her door. It was Quasimodo sleeping there upon the stones.

Meanwhile, Claude Frollo, by now having heard of Esmeralda's rescue, felt sick and locked himself in his own cell. He passed whole days with his face at the window. From this window, he could see Esmeralda's cell. He often saw her, with her goat—sometimes with Quasimodo. He asked himself what reason could have led Quasimodo to save her. Then he found himself jealous.

"It was bad enough when it was the captain; but this fellow!"

Since he knew the girl to be alive, he thought of her all the time. One night, unable to think about anything else, he leaped from his bed, threw a gown over his shirt and left his cell, lamp in hand.

He knew where to find the key to the door that led to her gallery and cell.

That night Esmeralda fell asleep in her cell. She had

been asleep for some time, dreaming, as she always did, of Phoebus, when she thought she heard a noise. She opened her eyes. The night was very dark. Still, she saw a face peering in at the window. When this face saw that Esmeralda was looking at it, it blew out the lamp.

"Oh," said she, "the priest!"

She was frozen with fear.

A moment after, she felt a touch. The priest had glided to her side. He clasped her in his arms.

"Leave, you monster! Go away, you murderer!" she said.

"Have mercy on me," said the priest. "If you knew what my love is for you!"

She shrieked, "Help! Help!"

No one came. Djali alone was awakened, and all it could do was bleat.

Suddenly, in her struggle, as she fought on the floor, the Gypsy's hand found something cold and metallic. It was Quasimodo's whistle. She grabbed it and raised it to her lips and blew with all her might. The whistle gave forth a sharp, shrill sound.

"What is that?" said the priest.

Almost as he spoke, he felt himself grasped in the dark by a strong arm. "Quasimodo!" he cried. He forgot that Quasimodo was deaf.

In a moment, the priest was stretched out on the floor, and felt a heavy knee pressed against his chest. Then Claude Frollo felt a huge hand drag him from the cell by the heels. Luckily for him, the moon had risen a few moments before. Its pale light fell upon the priest. Quasimodo looked him in the face, trembled, released his hold and shrank back.

The priest rushed down the stairs.

VIII

The Attack on Notre Dame

ONE DAY, as the author Pierre Gringoire was studying the sculptures in a chapel, he suddenly felt a hand on his shoulder. He turned. It was the archdeacon Claude Frollo. He found him quite changed—pale as snow, hollow-eyed, his hair almost white.

"Master Pierre," said the priest, "the Gypsy, your wife, took refuge in Notre Dame. But within three days justice will again overtake her, and she will be hanged in the Grève square. Parliament has issued an order to take her from the church."

"What harm does it do if a poor girl takes shelter in Notre Dame?" said Gringoire.

"There are devils in the world," said the priest, perhaps thinking of himself as one of their number. "But we must save her. Remember, she saved your life."

"Yes," said Gringoire, "that's so. I have a plan. The vagabonds are brave fellows. The Gypsy nation loves her! They will rise to rescue her at the suggestion. Nothing easier! They'll make a sudden attack and, in the middle of the confusion, she can be carried off. Tomorrow night."

"It is well," said the priest. "Until tomorrow, then."

The next evening, when the night bells were ringing

56

from every belfry in Paris, there was even more uproar than usual in the vagabonds' Court of Miracles. Numerous groups were chatting together, as if planning some great adventure. Here and there, some scamp squatted on the ground, sharpening a rusty iron blade.

Within the tavern, there was much drinking and card-playing. There were three main groups pressing around three people we have already met. One group encircled the Duke of the Gypsies, who sat upon a table talking about secrets of magic. Another mob crowded closely about the King of the Beggars and Thieves. Armed to the teeth, he was handing out piles of weapons—axes, swords, knives, arrows and crossbows. Even the children armed themselves, and there were also legless cripples, crawling about, with long swords at their sides.

The last group was the noisiest, jolliest and most numerous, and in the midst of them sat a young man in a heavy suit of armor—the archdeacon's brother, Jehan Frollo! His belt was full of daggers and knives, a huge sword hung at his side and a rusty crossbow was on the other leg.

"Today I wear armor for the first time. I'm a vagabond! We are about to go on a fine adventure. We'll take the church, break open the doors, carry off the lovely damsel in distress, save her from the judges, save her from the priests. Then we'll strip Notre Dame of its treasures. A short life and a merry one, I say!"

"Come!" called the King of Thieves, "hurry and arm yourselves! We march in an hour!"

"Poor Esmeralda!" said a Gypsy. "She's our sister. We must rescue her."

When the hour came, the king cried in a voice of thunder, "Midnight!"

At this word, all the vagabonds, men, women and children, rushed from the tavern, with a clatter of weapons. The king raised his voice, "Now, silence, as we pass through Paris! The torches shall not be lighted until we reach Notre Dame! Forward march!"

Minutes later the Paris watchmen fled in terror as they saw the long line of dark, silent men.

That same night, Quasimodo did not sleep. He had just made his last round of the church and given a glance at his poor, unused bells, when he climbed to the roof of the north tower and gazed out over Paris.

While his one eye roamed over the city, the hunchback felt within him a strange worry. For some days he had been upon his guard. He had constantly seen evil-looking men prowling about the church, never taking their eyes from the girl's hiding place. He therefore stationed himself upon his tower, keeping faithful watch, like a trusty dog, with a thousand doubts and fears.

At last, despite the darkness, he saw the first part of the vagrants' procession emerge into the square.

The idea of an attempt against the Gypsy girl came to his mind. Should he awaken her; help her to escape? Which way? The streets were full; the church backed up against the river. There was no boat! There was but one thing to be done—to die if need be on the threshold of Notre Dame; to resist at least until some help should come, if any there were, and not to disturb Esmeralda's sleep.

The crowd seemed to increase every moment in the square. Suddenly a light shone out, and in an instant seven or eight blazing torches rose above the heads of the multitude. Quasimodo then plainly saw the frightful mass of ragged men and women below him in the square,

armed with weapons, the blades of which glistened. Quasimodo picked up his lantern and went down to the platform between the towers to get a better view and to think
about a way to defend the girl.

The King of the Thieves commanded his vagabond
troops into order, and declared, "To you, Bishop of Paris, I,
the King of the Thieves, proclaim: 'Our sister, falsely
condemned for magic, has taken refuge in your church.
You owe her shelter and safety. Now, the Parliament
desires to take her back, and you have allowed this; so
that indeed she would be hanged tomorrow were not God
and the vagabonds here to help her. We have therefore
come here to you, O Bishop. If your church is sacred, our
sister is likewise sacred; if our sister is not sacred, neither
is your church.'"

Unfortunately, Quasimodo could not hear these words.
He still thought they were there to kill, not rescue,
Esmeralda.

The king announced, "Forward, boys! To your work,
vagabonds!"

Thirty strong men stepped into line with hammers and
crowbars. They advanced toward the main entrance of the
church, mounted the steps, and were soon crouching
beneath the arched doorway, working away at the door. A
crowd of vagrants followed them to help or encourage
them.

Suddenly, there was a tremendous crash. A huge log
had fallen from the sky; it had crushed a dozen of the
vagrants on the church steps, and had bounced off and
broken the legs of various others. The crowd scattered
with cries of terror.

The bandits, protected by the doorway, stood for several
moments staring into the air.

"It must be witchcraft!" growled the Duke of the Gypsies. "It must be the moon that flung that log at us."

Nothing could be seen on the front of the cathedral, to the top of which the light of the torches did not reach. The heavy piece of timber lay in the middle of the square, and loud were the groans of the men who had received its first crash.

"To work, I say, vagrants," shouted the King of the Thieves. "Force the door."

No one made a move.

"I swear," he said, "here's a pack of fellows who are afraid of a log!"

"King," said one of the men, "it's not the log that stops us; it's the door. We need a battering ram."

The king ran up to the log and set his foot upon it. "Here you have one," he exclaimed. "We've had it sent to us."

Soon the heavy log, lifted like a feather by two hundred sturdy arms, was hurled against the great door. At the shock of the log, the door boomed like a vast drum; the door did not break, but the whole cathedral shook.

At the same moment a shower of large stones began to rain from the top of the church upon the men of the battering ram.

But the men did not stop, despite the stones that cracked their skulls. The long beam still battered the door, like the clapper of a bell; the stones still rained down, and the door croaked and groaned.

Of course, the unexpected resistance that so angered the vagabonds came from Quasimodo.

When he had come down to the platform between the towers, his head whirled in confusion. He ran along the gallery, coming and going like a madman, looking down from above at the mass of vagabonds ready to rush upon the church. He thought of climbing the south belfry and ringing the alarm; but before he could have set the bell in motion, before big Marie's voice could utter a single tone, the church door might be broken into ten times. What was to be done?

He remembered that men had been at work all day repairing the wall, timbers and roof of the south tower.

Quasimodo flew to the tower. The lower rooms were indeed full of materials. There were piles of rough stones, sheets of lead in rolls, heavy sawn logs, heaps of plaster and rubbish.

There was no time to be lost. The hammers and crow-bars were at work below. With his strength increased by his sense of danger, he lifted one of the logs, the heaviest and longest that he could find; he shoved it through a window, over the edge of the short wall surrounding the platform. The enormous log, intended for the rafters, fell one hundred and sixty feet, scraping the wall, smashing the carvings, turning over and over several times. At last it reached the ground.

Quasimodo saw the vagabonds scatter as the log fell. He took advantage of their terror; and while they stared at the timber dropped from heaven, he silently collected plaster, stones and gravel, even the masons' bags of tools, upon the edge of that short wall from which the log had already been launched.

Thus, as soon as they began to batter at the door, the hail of stones began to fall, and it seemed to them as if the church were falling on their heads.

Besides the objects which he had piled upon the wall, he had collected a heap of stones on the platform itself. As soon as he was through with the first pile, he started with the one below. He stooped and rose, stooped and rose again; a huge stone fell, then another. Now and again he watched a particularly fine stone, and if it did its work well, he said, "Hmm!"

Meanwhile, the scoundrels were not discouraged. His shower of stones was not preventing their attack. He now observed, a little below the wall from which he was crushing the vagrants, two long stone gutters with spouts that emptied directly over the great door. An idea flashed upon his mind. He gathered rolls of lead and, having carefully laid this pile before the mouth of the two spouts, he set fire to it with his lantern.

During this time, the stones having stopped falling, the vagrants had stopped looking up. Like a pack of dogs that have hunted a wild boar to its lair, they crowded around the door. They awaited the final blow that would knock it through. Each one wanted to be the first to rush into that cathedral, in which were stored riches of three centuries. At this moment the crooks and thieves thought far less of freeing the Gypsy girl than they did of robbing Notre Dame.

Just as they gathered together about the battering ram for a final effort, a howl, more frightful even than that which had risen and died away from beneath the log, again burst in their midst. Those who did not shriek, those who still lived, looked up. Two streams of molten lead fell from the top of the building into the very thickest of the mob.

They fled every which way, tossing aside the log, running from the square.

All eyes were turned to the top of the church. Upon the top of the topmost gallery, higher than the central window, a vast flame rose between the two belfries. Below this

Two streams of molten lead fell from the top of the building into the very thickest of the mob.

flame, below the dark low wall, two spouts coming out of gargoyles were spewing out sheets of fiery rain.

The silence of terror came upon the vagabonds.

The leaders of the vagabonds withdrew and had a meeting.

The King of the Thieves muttered, "It's impossible!"

"It's an old witch of a church," said the Duke of the Gypsies. "Guillaume de Paris, who built this church, was a magician. Just look up there, it's a demon walking to and fro before the fire!"

"I'll swear!" said the King of the Thieves, "it's that damned bell-ringer; it's Quasimodo! Let's make one more try."

"We shall not enter by the door," said the Duke of the Gypsies. "We must find the weak spot in the old witch's armor."

"Who'll join us?" said the king.

Just then, Jehan Frollo, the archdeacon's brother, arrived, running as fast as was possible under the weight of his heavy armor and a long ladder which he dragged over the pavement.

"Victory!" shouted the young man. "Here's a ladder. Do you see that row of statues over there, above the three porches?"

"Yes," said the king. "What then?"

"At the end of that gallery is a door, and with this ladder I will climb to it, and then I am in the church."

Jehan dragged the ladder after him, shouting, "Help, lads, help!"

In an instant the ladder was lifted, and placed against the railing of the lower gallery, over one of the side doors. The crowd of vagrants, giving loud cheers, massed to the foot of it, eager to climb; but Jehan was the first to go up.

The journey was long and slow. The gallery was some eighty feet above the pavement. Jehan climbed carefully, slowed by his heavy armor, clinging to the ladder with one hand and his crossbow with the other.

The vagrants followed him. There was one on every rung. At last the student touched the balcony, and easily stepped over the short wall, amid the applause of the crowd. And so, as master of the heights, he shouted with joy. A moment later he was too frightened to move; behind one of the many statues on the gallery was Quasimodo, his glittering eye lurking in the shadow.

Before a second invader could set foot upon the gallery, the hunchback leaped to the side of the balcony, grabbed the ends of the two uprights of the ladder in his strong hands, raised them, and pushed them. Then the ladder plunged backward, for a moment stood tall, then tottered, then all at once fell headlong on the pavement with its cargo of bandits. Only a few miserable men managed to crawl away from under the heap of dead.

Jehan Frollo, for his part, was in a dreadful situation. He was alone in the gallery with the dreadful bell-ringer, parted from his companions by a high wall. While Quasimodo juggled with the ladder, the student hurried to the back door, which he supposed would be open. Not at all. The deaf man, on entering the gallery, had fastened it behind him. Jehan then hid himself behind a statue of a king, not daring to breathe, and eyeing the monstrous hunchback with terror.

For a few moments the deaf man paid no attention to him; but finally he turned his head and was surprised to see the student.

"Ho, ho!" said Jehan. "Why do you look at me with that sad single eye like that?" As he said this, he slyly adjusted the arrow on his crossbow. "Quasimodo," he cried, "I am going to change your name! From now on, rather than 'the one-eyed,' you shall be called 'the blind.'"

The arrow flew, whizzing through the air, and into the hunchback's left arm. It disturbed Quasimodo no more than a scratch would have disturbed one of the statues. He put his hand to the arrow, pulled it out and broke it across his knee; then he let the two pieces fall to the ground. Jehan had no time to fire a second shot. Quasimodo took a long breath, leaped like a grasshopper and came down upon the student, whose armor was flattened against the wall by the shock.

Then by the dim light of the torches a terrible thing might have been seen.

Quasimodo with his left hand grasped both Jehan's arms; with his right hand the deaf man removed from Jehan one piece of his armor after another. Quasimodo looked like a monkey picking a nut as he dropped the student's iron shell, bit by bit, at his feet.

When the youth found himself stripped, disarmed and helpless in those terrible hands, he did not try to speak to that deaf man, but he laughed in his face.

From below they saw Quasimodo standing upon the low wall, holding the boy with one hand, and swinging him round; then a sound was heard like a box made of bone dashed against a wall, and something fell, but caught a third of the way down upon a projection. It was a dead body which hung there, bent over, the back broken, the skull empty.

A cry of horror rose from the vagabonds.

"Vengeance!" yelled the king.

The poor student's death filled the mob with fury. In a few moments Quasimodo, in despair, saw that fearful swarm mounting on all sides to attack Notre Dame. Those who had no ladders had knotted ropes; those who had no ropes scrambled up the jutting sculptures. There was no way to resist this rising tide of awful figures. A layer of living monsters seemed to cover all the stone monsters of the cathedral front.

Meanwhile, the square was starred with a thousand torches. This scene of confusion was suddenly ablaze with light. The square cast a red glow upon the sky. The whole city seemed to be awake. Distant alarm-bells sounded. The vagabonds howled, panted, swore, climbed higher and higher; and Quasimodo, powerless against so many foes, shuddering for the Gypsy girl, seeing these faces come nearer and nearer to his gallery, prayed to Heaven for a miracle.

He had lost all hope of saving the Gypsy. He ran up and down the gallery. Notre Dame was about to be captured by the vagrants. Suddenly the gallop of horses filled the neighboring streets and, with a long train of torches and a company of horsemen riding at full speed with their lances lowered, the sound burst into the square like a tornado.

"Long live France! France! Soldiers, strike down these wretches! Phoebus de Châteaupers to the rescue!"

The terrified vagabonds wheeled about.

Quasimodo, who heard nothing, saw the swords, the torches, the horsemen, at whose head he noticed Captain Phoebus. He saw the confusion of the vagrants, and he derived so much strength from this unexpected help that he hurled from the church the foremost attackers, who were already coming over the gallery walls.

The vagabonds fought bravely; they defended themselves. They were caught between attacking Notre Dame and being attacked themselves.

The square was filled with thick smoke, which the flash of muskets streaked with fire.

At last the vagabonds gave up. They broke through the king's troops and fled in every direction, leaving the square heaped with bodies.

When Quasimodo, who had not stopped fighting for a single instant, saw this victory, he fell upon his knees and raised his hands to heaven; then, mad with joy, he ran, he climbed to that little cell, all access to which he had so well defended. He had but one thought now: that was, to kneel before the girl whom he had saved for the second time.

When he entered the cell, he found it empty!

IX

Esmeralda's Choice

WHEN THE VAGABONDS first attacked the church, Esmeralda was asleep.

Soon the ever-increasing noise around the building, and the worried bleating of her goat, which waked before she did, roused her from her slumbers. She sat up, listened, looked about; then, alarmed by the light and commotion, hurried from her cell to see what it all meant. The whole scene made her think of a weird battle waged by the spirits of witchcraft against the stone monsters of the church. She ran back to the cell and hid her head in the pillow.

Little by little, however, her fear changed. She imagined now that the mass of people must be coming to tear her from her cell and kill her. She lay on her bed trembling for a very long time.

Then she heard steps close by. She turned. Two men, one of whom carried a lantern, entered her cell. She uttered a shriek.

"Fear nothing," said a familiar voice. "It is I."

"Who?"

"Pierre Gringoire!"

That name calmed her fears. She raised her eyes and saw that it was indeed the author; but beside him stood a black-robed figure, his head covered with a hood.

The little goat, meanwhile, rubbed herself fondly against the playwright's knees. Gringoire petted her.

"Who is that with you?" said the Gypsy.

"A friend of mine. My dear girl, your life is in danger, and Djali's too. They still want to hang you. We are your friends and have come to save you. Follow us."

"Is it true?" cried Esmeralda.

"Yes, quite true," said Gringoire. "Come quickly."

"I will," she said. "But why doesn't your friend speak?"

"He was brought up to be silent, that's all."

Gringoire took her by the hand; his companion picked up the lantern and went on in front. The girl let them lead her away. The goat followed them with leaps of delight, it was so rejoiced to see Gringoire once more.

They rapidly went down the tower stairs, crossed the church, which was echoing with the noise outside, and came into a small courtyard. It was deserted. They made their way toward the door that led from this courtyard to the Terrain, an enclosed strip of ground forming the far eastern end of the island in the rear of the church. The man in black opened the door with a key. They found no one there. The sound of the vagrants' attack reached them more faintly. However, they were still very close to the danger.

The man with the lantern walked straight to the end of the Terrain. There, on the very edge of the water, was hidden a small boat. The man signed to Gringoire and Esmeralda to enter it. The goat followed them. The man stepped in last; then he cut the rope, shoved off from the shore and sat down with a pair of oars, rowing with all his strength toward the middle of the river.

The boat made its way slowly toward the right bank. The

girl watched the strange man with dread. His hood, still drawn over his head, formed a sort of mask over his face. He had not yet breathed a word. The only sound in the boat was that of the oars and the ripple of water against the sides of the boat.

The noise around Notre Dame was increasing. They paused and listened. They heard shouts of victory. All at once a hundred torches, which lit up the helmets of the soldiers, appeared upon all parts of the church. These torches seemed to be searching for someone or something. And soon distant cries of "The Gypsy! The witch! Death to the Gypsy!" fell on the ears of the people in the boat.

The girl hid her face in her hands, and the unknown boatman began to row for the Right Bank. A jolt warned them that the boat had reached shore. The uproar still went on from the City. The stranger got up, went to the Gypsy and tried to take her by the arm to help her to land. She pulled away from him, springing out of the boat without help. She stood for a moment watching the water as it glided by. And then she realized that she was alone upon the shore with the stranger. Gringoire, in his concern for his beloved Djali's safety and believing it safe to allow the stranger to take care of Esmeralda, had run off with the goat among the houses nearby.

Esmeralda felt the hand of the unknown man upon her arm. It was a cold, strong hand. He started walking with her rapidly toward the square of the Grève. She allowed him to drag her along, running while he walked.

She looked in every direction. Not a single passer-by. The shore was deserted.

The stranger pulled her on in the same silence and with the same speed. "Who are you?" Who are you?" she asked.

They came finally to a large open square. The moon shone faintly. They were in the Grève. In the middle stood a black cross: it was the gallows. She now knew where she was.

The man stopped, turned to her and lifted his hood.

"Oh!" she said, "I was sure it must be you."

In the moonlight, Claude Frollo looked like a ghost of himself.

"Listen," said he; and she trembled at the sound of that voice. "This is the Grève. Your life is in my hands. There is an order from Parliament that returns you to the scaffold. I have rescued you from the hangman's hands; but even now they are pursuing you. See!"

He stretched his hand toward the City. The noise drew nearer; soldiers were seen along the opposite shore with torches, shouting: "The Gypsy! Where is the Gypsy? Death! Death!"

"I love you," said the priest to Esmeralda. "Do not speak if you mean to tell me that you hate me. I will not let you say that again. I have saved you—I can save you further. Everything is ready. It is for you to choose."

He ran, making her run after him—for he did not loose his hold of her—and went straight to the gallows, and pointed to it.

"Choose between us," said he.

She tore herself from his grasp, and fell at the foot of the gallows, throwing her arms around it; then she half turned her lovely head, and looked at the priest over her shoulder. Claude Frollo remained motionless, his finger still pointed at the gallows, as if he were a statue.

At last the Gypsy said, "This gallows is less horrible to me than you are."

"Do you then have no feeling for me?" said the priest.

"Will you never forgive me? Will you always hate me? You do not even look at me! You are thinking of other things, perhaps, while I stand and talk to you, and both of us are teetering here on the edge of death! Do not talk to me of your Captain Phoebus! Do not tell me that you love me, only tell me that you will try; that will be enough, and I will save you. One word of kindness—but a single word!"

She answered: "I tell you that I belong to my Phoebus, the handsome Phoebus that I love! You, priest, are old! You are ugly! Leave me!"

"Then die!" he said.

She tried to run. He grabbed her and dragged her after him over the pavement to the corner of the Tour-Roland.

Reaching it, he turned to her and said, "For the last time—will you be mine?"

"No!"

Then he called in a loud voice, "Sister Gudule! Here is the Gypsy girl! Avenge yourself!"

The girl felt herself suddenly seized by the elbow. A skinny arm was thrust from a hole in the wall, and held her with an iron grip.

"Hold her!" said the priest. "It's the runaway Gypsy. Do not let her go. I will fetch the officers. You shall see her hanged."

A laugh from the other side of the wall replied, "Ha, ha, ha!" The Gypsy saw the priest leave in the direction of the bridge to Notre Dame. The tramp of horses was heard coming from that way.

The girl now recognized the woman as the one who hated her and shouted threats. With terror, she twisted herself in agony and despair; but the woman held her with amazing strength.

Esmeralda sank back, and the fear of death came over

her. She heard the sad laugh of the woman in the cell, as she whispered in her ear, "Ha, ha, ha! You shall be hanged!"

She turned, almost fainting, to the window, and saw through the bars the savage face of the nun.

"What have I done to you?" said Esmeralda.

Sister Gudule began to mumble in singsong, "Gypsy girl! Gypsy girl! Gypsy girl! What have you done to me, do you say? Well, listen, and I will tell you. I had a child! A pretty little girl! My Agnes. And then the Gypsies stole my child! That is what you have done to me."

"Alas! I probably was not even born then!"

"Oh, yes!" said the nun, "you must have been born. She would have been about your age! For fifteen years I have been in this hole; for fifteen years I have suffered; for fifteen years I have prayed. I tell you, it was the Gypsies who stole her from me. Have you a heart? Fancy what it is to have a child who plays at your knee; a child who sleeps in your arms. It is such a helpless, innocent thing! Well, that's what they took from me! Now it is my turn. Oh, how I would bite you, if the bars did not prevent me! They took her while she slept! Ah! Gypsy mothers, you took my child! Come, look at yours!"

Then she began to laugh. Dawn was coming. The gallows became more and more clear to their sight.

"Mercy, dear lady!" said Esmeralda. "You seek your child, and I seek my parents."

"Give me my little Agnes," said Sister Gudule. "You know not where she is? I will show you. Here's her shoe— all that is left to me. Do you know where the mate to it is? If you know, tell me."

So saying, with her other hand stretched through the bars, she showed the Gypsy the little pink shoe.

"My God! My God!" said the Gypsy. Esmeralda quickly opened the little bag she wore about her neck.

The Gypsy pulled out from the bag a tiny shoe precisely like the other. A strip of paper was fastened to the little shoe, upon which these words were written:

> When the mate to this you have espied,
>   Your mother's arms shall open wide.

Quick as a flash of lightning the recluse compared the two shoes, read the words and pressed her beaming face to the window-bars, exclaiming, "My daughter! My daughter!"

"Mother!" said the Gypsy.

The wall and the iron grating kept the two apart. "Oh, the wall!" cried the woman. "Oh, to see you and not to kiss you! Your hand! Your hand!"

The girl put her arm through the window. The poor mother poured out tears upon that hand.

Then suddenly the gray-haired woman began to shake the bars of her cell fiercely. The bars held firm. Then she brought from one corner a large stone, which served her as a pillow, and hurled it against the bars with such force that one of them broke. A second blow utterly destroyed the old iron crossbar. Then with both hands she pulled out and destroyed the fragments.

She now seized her daughter by the waist and dragged her into the cell.

"My daughter! My daughter!" she cried. "I've found my daughter! Here she is! You made me wait fifteen years, my good God, but it was to make her more beautiful for me! My little girl! Kiss me! Those good Gypsies! It is really you. Then that was why my heart leaped up within me every time you passed; and I thought it was hate! Forgive me,

*The girl put her arm through the window. The poor
mother poured out tears upon that hand.*

Agnes, forgive me. You thought me very cruel, didn't you? I love you. It was I who gave you those big eyes. All my beauty has left me and gone to you. Kiss me."

The girl repeated over and over, with great sweetness, "Mother!"

"Oh, my Lord God, I have found my child! But is it believable—this whole story? How happy we shall be!"

At this moment the cell rang with the clash of weapons from outside and the galloping feet of horses. The girl threw herself into her mother's arms.

"Save me, save me, mother! I hear them coming!"

"Heavens! What do you say? I had forgotten; you are being pursued! Why, what have you done?"

"I do not know," replied the girl, "but I am condemned to die."

"To die!" said Sister Gudule.

"Yes, Mother," said Esmeralda. "They mean to kill me. They are coming now to capture me. That gallows is for me! Save me!"

"Oh, no," said her mother. "Such things cannot be!"

A distant voice was heard, saying, "This way! The priest says that we shall find her at the Rat-Hole!"

In a low voice the mother said to the girl, "There are soldiers everywhere. You cannot go. They are coming; I will speak to them. Hide yourself in the corner; they will not see you. I will tell them that you have escaped."

At that instant the voice of the priest—that devilish voice—passed very close to the cell, shouting, "This way, Captain Phoebus de Châteaupers!"

At that name, Esmeralda, huddling in her corner, made a movement.

"Do not stir!" said her mother.

A large crowd of armed men and horses halted outside

the cell. The mother got up and placed herself before the window in such a way as to cut off all view of the room.

An officer in command came to the window.

"Old woman," he said, "we are looking for a witch, that we may hang her. We were told that you had her."

"If you mean a girl who was put into my hands just a while ago, I can only tell you that she bit me, and I let her go. Now leave me in peace."

At this moment, the mother and girl heard another officer's voice outside saying, "It is no business for a soldier to hang witches. The mob is still raging over there. I must leave here and rejoin my men."

This voice was that of Phoebus de Châteaupers.

Esmeralda jumped up before her mother could prevent her and ran to the window, crying, "Phoebus, help, my Phoebus!"

Phoebus was no longer there. He had just galloped off on his horse. But the first officer was not yet gone and he saw the Gypsy girl!

"Ha, ha!" he cried. "Old woman, surrender that girl. Why should you prevent that witch from being hanged?"

"Why? She is my daughter!"

"I am sorry," said the officer. "But we must have her."

When the mother heard the picks and shovels banging away at her window, she uttered an awful scream.

Meanwhile, although the sun had not yet risen, it was broad daylight. It was the hour when the windows of the earliest risers in the great city open. A few country people, fruit-sellers going to market on their donkeys, began to pass through the Grève; they paused a moment at the sight of this cluster of soldiers huddled in front of the Rat-Hole.

The mother had seated herself beside her daughter, covering her with her body. As the work of the men continued to destroy the wall under the window of her cell, the mother pressed the girl closer and closer. All at once she saw the wall quiver, and she heard the officer's voice urging the men on.

Now she spoke, cursing the soldiers: "This is horrible! You are robbers! Do you really mean to take my daughter away from me? Murderers! Help! Help! Will you take my child? Don't you know what it is to have a child of your own?"

The crowbars and picks finally brought down a block of stone under the window.

"Gentlemen, soldiers," Sister Gudule pleaded, "you will not take my dear little one from me!"

The hangman and his men entered the cell. The Gypsy saw the soldiers coming.

"My mother!" she cried. "My mother! They are coming!"

The mother held her closely in her arms and covered her with kisses.

The hangman seized the girl. When Esmeralda felt his hand she shrieked and fainted. He tried to loosen her mother's hold, she having wrapped her hands around her daughter's waist; it was impossible to separate the women. The hangman therefore dragged the girl from the cell, and her mother after her. The mother's eyes were also closed.

At this moment the sun rose, and there was already a large crowd of people in the square, looking on from a little distance to see who was being dragged in this way over the pavement to the gallows.

Far off, on the top of the Notre Dame tower overlooking the Grève, two men were to be seen darkly outlined against the clear morning sky, apparently watching this scene.

The hangman paused with his burden at the foot of the

fatal ladder, and there he passed his rope around the girl's neck. Esmeralda opened her eyes and saw the gallows above her head. She cried, "No, no!" Her mother, whose head was buried and lost in her child's clothes, did not speak a word; but she kissed her daughter again and again. The hangman took advantage of this moment to unclasp the woman's arms from the prisoner. Then he took the girl upon his shoulder, and put his foot upon the ladder to go up.

At this instant the mother, crouching on the pavement, opened wide her eyes. She sprang up with a terrible look; then, like a wild beast leaping upon its prey, she threw herself upon the hangman's hand, and bit it. It was a flash of lightning. The hangman yelled with pain. They ran to his aid. With some trouble they pulled his bleeding hand out from between the mother's teeth. The men pushed her away; her head fell heavily to the pavement. They lifted her up; she fell back again. She was dead.

The hangman, who had not let go his hold of the girl, continued his climb up the ladder.

X

Quasimodo's Revenge

BACK WHEN Quasimodo saw that the cell was empty, the Gypsy gone, that while he was defending her she had been carried off, he tore his hair, and stamped with rage and surprise; then he ran from end to end of the church in search of his princess, uttering strange howls as he went, scattering his red hair upon the floor.

It was just at that moment that the soldiers entered Notre Dame in triumph, also in search of the Gypsy. Quasimodo helped them, without suspecting—poor deaf fellow!—that they wanted to kill her. But they could not find her.

After the soldiers left, twenty, no, a hundred times Quasimodo made the rounds of the church, from one end to the other, from top to bottom, upstairs, downstairs, running, calling, crying, sniffling, poking his head into every hole, thrusting a torch into every vault, desperate, mad.

Finally, when he was sure, very sure, that she was no longer there, that she had been stolen from him, he slowly climbed the tower stairs. The church was again deserted, and was silent. The soldiers had left it to track the witch into the City. Quasimodo, alone in that vast cathedral, so crowded and so noisy but a short time ago, returned to the room where the Gypsy had for so many weeks slept under his watchful care.

As he came to the cell, he imagined that he might perhaps find her there. But of course the cell was still empty. The unhappy deaf man slowly walked around it, lifted the bed and looked under it, as if she might be hidden between the mattress and the stones; then he shook his head and stood staring stupidly. All at once he trampled his torch under his foot and, without a word, he threw himself headlong against the wall and fell fainting on the floor.

When he came to his senses, he dragged himself from the cell on his knees, and crouched before the door, staring back into the cell. And in this pose he remained for an hour, sad and thoughtful. It was then that he wondered who could have been the kidnapper of the Gypsy. He remembered the priest's midnight attack on the girl. He remembered his own attack—with the priest—months before, and soon knew without a doubt that Claude Frollo had stolen the Gypsy from him. Such, however, were his respect, gratitude, devotion and love for the priest that the thirst for blood and murder which he would have felt for any other were turned to more sadness.

Just as he was thinking in this way about the priest, as dawn arrived, he saw on the upper story of Notre Dame a moving figure. It was the archdeacon! Claude Frollo was going toward the north tower; but his face was turned aside toward the right bank of the Seine, and he held his head still, as if trying to see something over the roofs. The priest passed above Quasimodo without seeing him.

Quasimodo got up and followed the archdeacon. He climbed the tower stairs, meaning to go to the top, to learn why Claude Frollo was there. When he reached the top of the tower, he looked to see where the priest was. Claude

Frollo stood with his back to him. There is a short wall around the platform of the belfry tower; the priest, whose eyes were set upon the right bank, leaned over the railing that overlooks the Notre Dame bridge.

Quasimodo, quietly coming up behind him, looked out to see what the priest was watching so closely. The priest did not hear the deaf man beside him; his gaze was centered on a single point.

Quasimodo followed the direction of the priest's glance, and in this way the eye of the poor deaf man fell upon the Grève square. He saw what the priest was watching. The ladder was standing against the gallows. There were people in the square and a number of soldiers. A man dragged across the pavement a white object to which something black was fastened. This man stopped at the foot of the gallows.

At this point something happened which Quasimodo could not quite make out. Not because his one eye had lost its power, but there was a cluster of soldiers that prevented him from seeing everything. Besides, at this moment the sun rose, and such a flood of light burst from the horizon that it seemed every roof and church-top was set on fire at once.

Meanwhile, the man continued to climb the ladder. Then Quasimodo saw him again clearly. He had a woman across his shoulder—a girl dressed in white; this girl had a knotted rope around her neck. Quasimodo recognized her.

It was Esmeralda!

The man reached the top of the ladder. There he arranged the noose.

Here the priest, to see the better, knelt upon the short wall.

All at once the man pushed the ladder quickly from him with his heel; and Quasimodo, who had hardly breathed for several moments past, saw the poor girl dangling from one end of the rope, a dozen feet from the ground. Quasimodo saw a horrible shudder run through the Gypsy's body. The priest, on his part, with outstretched neck and starting eyes, watched that dreadful scene.

A devilish laugh broke from the lips of the archdeacon. Quasimodo did not hear this laughter, but he saw it.

The bell-ringer pulled back a few feet from the arch-deacon, and then, suddenly rushing upon him with his huge hands, he hurled Claude Frollo into the air.

The priest cried, "Damnation!" and fell.

The gutter just below the short wall stopped his fall. He clung to it with his hands, and, as he opened his mouth for a second shriek, he saw, looking over the edge of the wall, above his head, the terrible, avenging face of Quasimodo.

Then he was silent.

There was nothing beneath him. A fall of more than two hundred feet—and the pavement.

Quasimodo had only to stretch out his hand to save Claude Frollo, his adopted father; but he did not even look at him. The deaf man looked at the Grève square; he looked at the gallows; he looked at the Gypsy girl. He leaned his elbows on the railing, in the very place where the archdeacon had been a moment ago, and there, never moving his eye from the only object that at this time existed for him, he stood motionless and silent as if struck by lightning, and a river of tears flowed from that eye which until then had cried but a single tear.

Meanwhile, the archdeacon gasped. His bald head streamed with sweat, his fingernails bled against the stone. He heard his robe, by which he hung to the gutter spout, crack and rip at every jerk that he gave it. This spout ended in a lead pipe, which was bending beneath the weight of his body.

The archdeacon felt the pipe slowly giving way. He looked down below him into the square; when he raised his head his eyes were shut and his hair was standing up. He clung there, hugging the gutter, hardly breathing, not moving. Little by little, however, his fingers slipped from the spout; the weakness of his arms and the weight of his body increased more and more. Every moment the gutter that supported him bent a bit nearer to the emptiness.

He saw below him a fearful sight—a roof as small as a card bent in half. He gazed at the sculptures on the tower, like him hanging over the edge; all around him was stone: before his eyes, these gaping, sculpted monsters; below, far down in the square, the pavement; above his head, Quasimodo weeping.

At last the archdeacon, in a rage and fright, knew that it was all over. However, he called up his final bit of strength for a last try. He braced himself against the gutter, set his knees against the wall, hooked his hands into a chink in the stones, and managed to climb up perhaps a foot; but this struggle made the pipe upon which he hung bend suddenly. With the same effort his robe tore apart. The poor man's trembling hands let go of the gutter. He fell.

Quasimodo watched him fall.

At first he fell downward, with outstretched arms; then he rolled over and over several times; the wind blew him to the roof of a house, where he broke some of his bones. Still he was not dead when he landed there. The bell-ringer saw him make another try to catch the peak of the roof with his fingernails, but the slope was too steep, and his strength was gone. He slid quickly down the roof, like a loose tile, and fell to the pavement. He no longer moved.

Quasimodo then raised his eye to the Gypsy, whose body he could see, as it swung from the gallows; then he again lowered it to the archdeacon, stretched at the foot of the tower, and he said, with a sob, "Oh, all that I ever loved!"

Toward the evening of the same day, when the bishop's officers came to remove the body of the archdeacon from the pavement, Quasimodo had vanished from Notre Dame. Indeed, he was never seen again; no one knew what became of him.

During the night following the hanging of Esmeralda, the hangman's assistants took down her body from the gallows and carried it, as was customary, to the graveyard at Montfaucon, about a quarter of a mile from the walls of Paris. Imagine, at the top of a chalk-hill, a platform upon which stood sixteen huge pillars of stone. At regular points from these pillars hung chains; and from all these chains swung skeletons. This was Montfaucon.

As for the strange disappearance of Quasimodo, all that we have been able to discover is this. Two years or so after the events that close this story, among all those bodies, two skeletons were found locked in close embrace. One of the two, that of a woman, still had about its neck a necklace, with a little silk bag, which was open and empty. The other skeleton, which held this one in so close an embrace, was that of a man. It was noticed that his spine was curved, his head close between his shoulder blades, and one leg shorter than the other. Moreover, his neck was not broken, and it was clear that he had not been hanged. The man to whom these bones belonged must therefore have come there himself and died there. When an attempt was made to loosen him from the skeleton that he clasped, he crumbled into dust.

THE END

☆DOVER☆
CHILDREN'S THRIFT CLASSICS

Just $1.00
All books complete and unabridged, except where noted.
96pp., 5³/₁₆″ × 8¼″, paperbound.

AESOP'S FABLES, Aesop. 28020-9

THE LITTLE MERMAID AND OTHER FAIRY TALES, Hans Christian Andersen. 27816-6

THE UGLY DUCKLING AND OTHER FAIRY TALES, Hans Christian Andersen. 27081-5

THE THREE BILLY GOATS GRUFF AND OTHER READ-ALOUD STORIES, Carolyn Sherwin Bailey (ed.). 28021-7

THE STORY OF PETER PAN, James M. Barrie and Daniel O'Connor. 27294-X

ROBIN HOOD, Bob Blaisdell. 27573-6

THE ADVENTURES OF BUSTER BEAR, Thornton W. Burgess. 27564-7

THE ADVENTURES OF CHATTERER THE RED SQUIRREL, Thornton W. Burgess. 27399-7

THE ADVENTURES OF DANNY MEADOW MOUSE, Thornton W. Burgess. 27565-5

THE ADVENTURES OF GRANDFATHER FROG, Thornton W. Burgess. 27400-4

THE ADVENTURES OF JERRY MUSKRAT, Thornton W. Burgess. 27817-4

THE ADVENTURES OF JIMMY SKUNK, Thornton W. Burgess. 28023-3

THE ADVENTURES OF PETER COTTONTAIL, Thornton W. Burgess. 26929-9

THE ADVENTURES OF POOR MRS. QUACK, Thornton W. Burgess. 27818-2

THE ADVENTURES OF REDDY FOX, Thornton W. Burgess. 26930-2

THE SECRET GARDEN, Frances Hodgson Burnett. (abridged) 28024-1

PICTURE FOLK-TALES, Valery Carrick. 27083-1

THE STORY OF POCAHONTAS, Brian Doherty (ed.). 28025-X

SLEEPING BEAUTY AND OTHER FAIRY TALES, Jacob and Wilhelm Grimm. 27084-X

THE ELEPHANT'S CHILD AND OTHER JUST SO STORIES, Rudyard Kipling. 27821-2

HOW THE LEOPARD GOT HIS SPOTS AND OTHER JUST SO STORIES, Rudyard Kipling. 27297-4

MOWGLI STORIES FROM "THE JUNGLE BOOK," Rudyard Kipling. 28030-6

NONSENSE POEMS, Edward Lear. 28031-4

BEAUTY AND THE BEAST AND OTHER FAIRY TALES, Marie Leprince de Beaumont and Charles Perrault. 28032-2

A DOG OF FLANDERS, Ouida (Marie Louise de la Ramée). 27087-4

PETER RABBIT AND 11 OTHER FAVORITE TALES, Beatrix Potter. 27845-X